Sandy Paws

Dogs and Cats on Delmarva

Nancy Sakaduski, Editor

Nancy Powichroski Sherman, Associate Editor

Cat & Mouse Press
Lewes, DE 19958
www.catandmousepress.com

Cover illustration by Sara England Designs. ©2020 Sara England, Inc.
Photo for "Beautiful Disaster" by Adrianne C. Lasker. ©2020 Adrianne C. Lasker.
Photo for "Courage" by Meg Ellacott. ©2020 Margaret Ellacott.
Photo for "My Daughter Teaches Every Child She Knows to Love Her Cat" by
Alice Morris. ©2020 Alice Morris. Art by Sarah Morris.
Photo for "For the Love of Dave" by Kathy Maas. ©2020 Kathy Maas.
Photo for "The Ginger" by Linda Chambers. ©2020 Linda Huntly Chambers.
Photo for "Running with Joey" by Sherri Wright. ©2020 Sherri Wright.
Photo for "St. Peter's Magic Cat" by Terri Clifton. ©2020 Terri Clifton.

Reprinted with permission:
"Beautiful Disaster," Adrianne C. Lasker. ©2020 Adrianne C. Lasker.
"The Case of the Lost Lhasa," Doug Harrell. ©2020 Douglas Gaines Harrell.
"Courage," Meg Ellacott. ©2020 Margaret Ellacott.
"Falling Into Place," Nancy Powichroski Sherman. ©2020 Nancy Powichroski
Sherman.
"Finding Sunshine," Robin Hill-Page Glanden. ©2020 Robin Page Glanden.
"Fireworks," Katherine Melvin. ©2020 Katherine Melvin.
"For the Love of Dave," Kathy Maas. ©2020 Kathy Maas.
"The Ginger," Linda Chambers. ©2020 Linda Huntly Chambers.
"The Heart Bandit," Jeanie P. Blair. ©2020 Jean Pitrizzi Blair.
"It Happened One Night," D.M. Domosea. ©2020 Dora M. Sears.
"Meanderings with Maisie," Mary Dolan. ©2020 Mary Irene Dolan.
"Midnight's Treasures," Doretta Warnock. ©2020 Doretta Warnock.
"My Daughter Teaches Every Child She Knows to Love Her Cat," Alice
Morris. ©2020 Alice Morris.
"The Private Diary of Pippi," Carolyn Fogerty. ©2020 Carolyn Fogerty.
"Running with Joey," Sherri Wright. ©2020 Sherri Wright.
"Saving Matilda," Susan Miller. ©2020 Suzanne Miller.
"St. Peter's Magic Cat," Terri Clifton. ©2020 Terri Clifton.
"Sometimes You Just Have to Dive In," Lonn Braender. ©2020 Lonn Braender.
"Three Dog Night," Kathaleen L. McCormick. ©2020 Kathaleen L. McCormick.
"Trooper," Chris Jacobsen. ©2020 Christiana Jacobsen.
"Zen," Tara A. Elliott. ©2020 Tara A. Elliott.

"My Daughter Teaches Every Child She Knows to Love Her Cat" by Alice
Morris was first published online by Silver Birch Press, (Lost and Found Poetry
and Prose Series).

"Running with Joey" by Sherri Wright was previously published in *Mojave
River Review*, Fall/ Winter, 2018.

About the cover: Sara England's original art is witty, whimsical, and wonderful.
While her art is sold around the world, Sara chose Rehoboth Beach to set up
shop. Please visit The Ruff Life on Baltimore Avenue.

Acknowledgments

This book would not have existed were it not for Irene Fick, who not only has great talent as a poet (check out her work!), but also has great ideas, one of which was for us to do an anthology of cat and dog stories. It was a great idea, as I'm sure you will agree when you dive into this delightful collection of stories and verse.

I would also like to thank my associate editor, Nancy Powichroski Sherman, who helped me with the difficult job of choosing the stories and poems, acted as a sounding board throughout the book's development, and put her excellent editing eye to work by proofreading the final manuscript.

I would also like to thank the volunteer readers who gave input that helped us with the selection of the stories and poems: Ellen Collins, Irene Fick, Cindy Hall, and Cynthia Myers.

Thank you all for giving so generously of your valuable time.

Contents

Trooper

by Chris Jacobsen

*T*he sand was everywhere, all the time. In her clothes, her hair, her bed, sometimes even her teeth. How did the locals stand it?

Six more months to go before she completed her third and final deployment to the Middle East. And then home. Jenna shook her head at the irony of leaving one sandy place for another. However, the gritty sands of Afghanistan could not hold a flare to the fine sands of the Delaware beaches.

Jenna pulled into the driveway of her grandmother's Lewes home under a cerulean sky on an early day in June. Jenna had been a military brat until her teens, when her father was sent to Germany. Instead of yet another move, she chose to live with Gram so she could stay at the same high school for all four years and develop lasting friendships.

She sat for a few minutes looking through the windshield, her mind awash with questions and doubts. Was she really done with the army? Could she handle civilian life again? How strange to once again be in charge of her daily agenda.

She grabbed her duffel and knocked on the door. Even though her grandmother was expecting her homecoming, Jenna thought it best to announce her arrival politely.

"Well, my, my," Gram said. "Welcome home. Come in!" She threw her arms open.

"It's so good to see you, Gram!" Jenna hugged the elderly woman as she looked around the living room, a place she had not seen for several years. The wicker furniture and yellowed linoleum floor showed their age. But it was home.

"Turn around and let me look at you. You're skin and bones, child."

"Not once I start eating your delicious cooking again." Both women laughed.

"I'll start dinner while you get settled."

Jenna unpacked her things in her old room. Her fresh eyes took note of the double bed with the fraying powder-blue chenille bedspread, the small dresser with a mirror above, and a lamp that had a lighthouse as its base. It seemed like a lifetime ago that she had looked upon this as her sanctuary. Slowly, she opened the drawers of the dresser, unsure of what they still held of her belongings. She flicked the light off and on, as if the blinking of the bulb could offer her safe passage like the lighthouse out in the bay did for passing ships. If only.

Jenna stepped into the shower and closed the door. She placed both hands on the tile wall and bent her head down, allowing the pulsating needles of hot water to penetrate her body like the fingers of a masseuse. Never before had she thought of this as a luxury. She dried off, changed into clean clothes, and ran her fingers through her towel-dried dark hair.

"Dinner smells great." Jenna said, entering the kitchen. "Here, let me make the salads." She rinsed off the cucumber and tomato and began to chop.

Gram took the roast from the oven to let it rest. "I thought you would be arriving with someone else."

Jenna glanced at her grandmother with a frown.

"Where's your dog?"

"We've got a surgery," Jenna yelled, as she pushed past Tyrone, a body builder from New Jersey, to approach the triage unit of the compound. A nurse hurried to greet her. Other troops jumped up while asking for details of the victim and injury.

"A gangrenous leg on a bitch, and I don't mean Jenna," quipped Tyrone.

Laughter erupted as Jenna scowled at her comrade. She excused Tyrone's gallows humor, knowing it was a way to stay sane when under life-and-death circumstances. She gently handed over the patient to be whisked into the operating theater. Bald patches pitted the buff-colored fur of the dog; skin cratered between the ribs like the rippling of desert dunes.

"*She* is a dog we found on the side of the road. Shallow breathing, unresponsive. Maybe a year old, about twenty pounds."

Harrison, a career surgeon with the army, visually assessed the front right leg of the sedated patient on his surgical table. He used his long, gloved fingers to clean away the caked-on grit of dried blood and sand. He took his time giving this patient the same level of care he would give any of his soldiers.

After what seemed to Jenna an excruciatingly long time, Harrison came to speak to the group. "Here's your culprit—a piece of shrapnel." He held up the large fragment for all to see. "The bone was shattered and, in addition to the gangrene, the leg had to go." Jenna's heart dropped.

Once the dog was released from recovery, Jenna stroked the pup while envisioning the difficult road ahead; not only would her body have to heal, but also she would have to learn a whole new way of walking.

"Well, Gram," Jenna said as she stabbed a forkful of salad, "I'll be picking her up next month if all goes well. Transporting dogs through border control is dicey, but once they enter, a safe-haven quarantine starts. Then, by the grace of the guy who started this rescue, the dogs are flown here to the states for adoption." Jenna poked at her baked potato. "I made sure they understood which one was earmarked for me."

"The poor dear." Gram reached across the table and patted Jenna's hand. "How sweet of you to adopt her. It will be good to have a dog in the house again. It's been six years since Tidewater died. I still miss that goofy little schnauzer."

Jenna sighed and again ran her fingers through her damp hair. "There are so many strays over there, and the desert is so harsh. I wish I could adopt them all."

"Well, let's stay focused on the positive. Thanks to you, one of them will have a loving home."

"And thanks to you, too. I really appreciate you letting her live with us." Jenna stood to clear the table and began washing the dishes. "I can't wait to see her again."

"What did you name her?"

"We need to name this brave girl," Jenna called out to her fellow soldiers.

"'Sniper!'" someone rang out.

"'Killer!'" guffawed the Texan.

"'Beast!'" blurted another from across the room.

"Knock it off," Jenna yelled. "She's been through a lot and her name should reflect that."

"Jenna's absolutely right," said Tyrone. "The name should be dignified and worthy of her status. How about 'Tripod'? Get it? Three legs!" He busted out laughing and others joined in.

"Screw you, Ty. You're such an asshole," Jenna said. "I'm serious. She's been a real trooper and I want to honor that." Jenna's eyes widened and a big smile crossed her lips. "That's it! Her name is 'Trooper'."

And so, Trooper began her rehab with a new identity. With proper medical care and two squares a day, she started to fill out her skin with barely a rib showing. The squad helped her learn to balance herself on three legs by placing a towel under her belly and having a soldier hold each side taut to support her weight. Day by day her hobbling became a bit steadier as she learned to walk on her remaining legs.

While waiting for Trooper to join her, Jenna floundered in her new role as a civilian. Having time on her hands seemed to heighten the stress and anxiety of having been in a war zone. She needed to acclimate herself before looking for a job, so she went for walks, read books, and stayed away from the news. While overseas, she couldn't wait to get back to the Lewes sand, but now that she was home, she couldn't bring herself to go to the beach. Just the thought of it made her tense.

Gram tried to coax her into going to Bingo on Wednesday nights and church on Sundays. "Oh, and Ivy Kershaw invited us to dinner when her grandson visits. He's about your age, so Ivy thought it would be nice for the two of you to meet."

Jenna let out a sigh. "I can't promise, Gram."

Now that she was master of her day, Jenna felt adrift. Where was the structure, the focus, the accomplishment? Although she didn't want to interact with neighbors, she found that she missed the tight connection with her squad. She knew if Tyrone were here, he would tell her to get off her butt and get her head back in the game. But he wasn't here. She needed someone who understood what she'd been through.

Trooper. She needed Trooper.

The sky was overcast that first morning in July when Jenna climbed into her car for the drive up I-95 to JFK airport, where she would finally collect her dog. She was nervous about their reunion. Would Trooper remember her? Associate Jenna with her painful past?

Jenna heard the barking before she saw the crates, each with a canine occupant. There she was! Trooper's tail started thumping against the travel crate as soon as she saw Jenna.

"Welcome home, soldier." Jenna knelt down to open the crate, prepared to give a reassuring hug, and instead received an enthusiastic face-licking. As she clipped on a collar with a pink camouflage design and attached the matching leash, she noticed Trooper seemed accustomed to life on three legs. All the way back to Lewes Jenna assured Trooper how life was going to be better for each of them now that they were together.

Jenna felt more at ease when she ventured outside with Trooper. They went for daily walks, and Trooper's three legs kept pace with Jenna's two. Sometimes Jenna drove them into the historical part of town. As long as she was with Trooper, she was able to cope with crowds such as the influx of tourists who, taking a break from the beach, enjoyed the history behind the Cannonball House or investigated the many eclectic gift shops.

She had hoped to take Trooper to the Lewes Unleashed Dog Park, but it was a private concern that required an annual membership fee. Jenna applied, but the new fiscal year started September first, so for the foreseeable future, her pooch still needed to be attached to her.

Jenna pondered the obstacle that still loomed ahead: going to the beach. Recalling the desert sand, she longed to feel the silkiness of the Lewes sand, to sit and drizzle handful after handful over her knees and wriggle her toes out of sight. Why was she so apprehensive?

She wanted to see Trooper's paws sink in the forgiving grains. In her mind's eye, Trooper frolicked like an exuberant puppy, tongue hanging out one side of her mouth, always turning her head to make sure she kept Jenna in sight. But what would her real reaction be? Did dogs have intrusive thoughts like humans? Would the grains beneath the dog's feet cause her to associate the Lewes beach with the coarse sand of her previous life? Would it make her relive her battle to stay alive?

There was only one way to find out.

They would go to Cape Henlopen State Park with Gram's season pass. The swimming and sunbathing beaches were off limits, but the surfing beach was fair game as long as dogs were on a leash. And, of course, as long as the owners came equipped with plastic bags for picking up any souvenirs the canines chose to leave behind.

Jenna parked the car and attached Trooper's leash. As soon as they stepped onto the sand, Trooper stopped. With a whimper, she circled Jenna's legs and pulled to go back to the car.

"It's OK, Troop, I'm nervous too. Why don't we just sit here for a bit?" Jenna bent down and scratched Trooper's ears. She led the dog several yards to the side of the path to allow others to pass. She sat down and encouraged Trooper to do the same.

Trooper's head ping-ponged back and forth as she scoped out her environment, detecting the level of safety. Jenna continued to speak in soothing tones, hoping to calm her dog as well as herself. They both watched as a young man came over the dune with his German shepherd mix. Jenna thought she saw the man catch sight of Trooper's missing limb. Funny, Jenna gave little thought to her sidekick's handicap because the pup navigated so well. Yes, she was slower than she would be if she had all four legs, but she got along just fine. Jenna wondered if Trooper remembered walking on all fours.

"We're OK, Troop. It's just going to take time, but we'll both get there. I promise."

"That's it, Troop. You're doing it! Come on. Just a bit farther."

Each day, Jenna or one of the other soldiers would run Trooper through her rehab paces. Not wanting the other leg muscles to atrophy, the sessions had started soon after surgery. For the first seven days, she had several brief sessions just to get her up and standing. Careful documentation was kept, at Jenna's insistence. The following week, an additional session was thrown in, along with encouragement to stand a bit longer and go a few steps farther.

Trooper generally complied with what was expected of her, but Jenna insisted that if Trooper was having an off day, they end the session early. The squad cheered Trooper through some tough adjustments but ones that would give her some sense of normalcy. Eventually, she developed her own lopsided gait.

At the end of every day, Jenna was there with words of praise and love.

The pair remained on the sand for a while as Jenna scooped up the tiny grains and poured them over Trooper's flank, telling her how glad she was that they were finally here. Needing a break, they got up and walked back to the car. Jenna got out the dog bowl and gave Trooper a drink, as she chugged water from her thermos. They made a loop around the parking lot several times and then headed back to their previous spot. Trooper hopped along contentedly until they again neared the sand.

Jenna continued to walk to see what resistance she would get from her dog. Trooper's hobble was a bit more pronounced on the shifting sand, but they covered more ground this time and soon sat down again.

"Troop, I know this is a bit scary; it's scary for me, too, but we'll take it slow. Each day a bit farther than before, OK?"

An hour later, headed back to the parking lot, they saw the man with the German shepherd. He paused, sensing his dog wanted to greet Trooper, who immediately threw up her guard. One word from his owner and the shepherd obediently sat down.

"Sorry to disturb you," said the man dressed in shorts and a yellow T-shirt, his hazel eyes shaded by a Blue Rocks baseball cap. "I'm Colin and this is Guinness."

Jenna held her hand along her forehead to block the sun from her eyes. Colin was tall, with light-brown hair and an open countenance. She reached out to shake his hand. "I'm Jenna and this is Trooper. She's not a fan of sand so we're taking it slowly."

"Baby steps, as they say."

"That definitely applies in this instance."

"Well, have a good rest of your day. Come on, Guinness."

As the pair headed back to the parking lot, Jenna noticed the green camouflage leash and wondered whether the owner was also a veteran or just liked the macho pattern.

Jenna and Trooper arrived back at the house. Gram, kneeling on the ground, looked up from under the brim of her sun hat and brushed dirt from her gardening gloves.

"Did you enjoy your afternoon at the beach?"

"*Enjoy* might be a bit of an optimistic word, but yes, I'm glad we went."

"Very nice. By the way, Mrs. Kershaw has asked us to dinner next Friday at six. May I tell her we will both be there?"

Jenna did not want to burden Gram with her anxiety. As far as Gram knew, the slow reintroduction to the beach was due solely to Trooper's apprehension. Although she had no desire to make small talk with an elderly neighbor and her grandson, she didn't want to disappoint Gram.

"Sure, that would be nice, Gram. I'll pick up some wine to take with us."

"Oh, yes, please do. I plan to bake a pie."

Honoring the house rule, dog and owner walked around to the back door so they didn't track sand through the house. Jenna removed her shoes and brushed off Trooper's paws.

In her bedroom, Jenna grabbed her notebook and made another entry. She was approaching Trooper's rehab here just like she did overseas, day-by-day sessions with hoped-for progress.

The next day they repeated their trip to the beach and picked their way farther from the dune and closer to the water. Jenna hoped that seeing other dogs running with their owners might encourage Trooper to do the same, but evidently it was too soon.

"Hello again," came a voice behind Jenna. She turned to see Colin and Guinness. "I see progress is being made."

"A bit. At this rate, it might take until Labor Day before we reach the ocean." Jenna laughed as she nervously ran her fingers through her windblown hair.

"Well, just FYI, Guinness is a service dog. He goes everywhere with me. If it weren't for him, I wouldn't be on this beach."

"I can relate to that."

"If we can be of any help, please just say the word."

"Thank you."

Colin and Guinness continued toward the ocean and Guinness fell in with another dog, jumping and barking a greeting. Jenna watched for longer than she cared to admit.

Thank you? Why didn't I say more to him, ask him about the leash? Am I not ready for even a causal relationship? Jenna continued to berate herself for being closed off to the kindness being offered to her and Trooper.

Jenna and her sidekick returned to the dog beach the following afternoon. They increased their distance again. Jenna thought Trooper would have an easier time walking on the wet sand since it was firmer than the dry, but the dog pulled back on the leash when she reached the edge of her comfort zone.

"Baby steps, right, girl?" Jenna lowered herself next to her pooch.

She didn't see Colin and his dog that day or the next. *I guess he read my reluctance and is avoiding me. I missed a shot at making a friend.*

Friday rolled around and Jenna found herself helping Gram roll out dough for two pies.

"Are you doing alright?" asked Gram. "You've been a bit quiet these past few days."

"Yeah, I'm OK. I just want Trooper to be able to let go of her fears." *And I wish I could, too.*

"Well, I'm going to change my clothes." Gram hung up her apron. "We can walk down to Ivy's as soon as the pies come out of the oven. Let's not forget the wine."

Jenna took a quick shower and applied blush and lipstick. She took the time to blow-dry her hair rather than going to dinner with a wet head.

"So long, Troop. You be a good girl. We'll be back soon."

The two women strolled down the sidewalk with their meal contributions in hand. Jenna smiled inwardly at the old-fashioned scenario in which she found herself.

Gram knocked on the door. Ivy Kershaw opened it with a warm invitation to come inside. "How lovely to see you again, Jenna. It has been quite some time, and I thank you for your service."

"Why are you using a cane?" inquired Gram.

"Oh, silly me. I fell a few days ago. Luckily, I didn't break a hip, but I sure did bruise it."

Jenna heard a familiar sound coming from the kitchen— the click of nails on linoleum. A moment later, a large dog made a beeline for Jenna, tail wagging and tongue out.

"Guinness?"

Colin came through the doorway. He greeted Gram and then turned to Jenna. "Hey, good to see you again. I didn't get to the beach the past few days because of Ivy's fall. And I didn't learn until tonight exactly who the dinner guests were." His eyes sparkled. "I'm very glad it's you."

Jenna's heart raced. "Colin. What a surprise." *Do not blush,* Jenna demanded of herself, as her cheeks flamed.

After dinner, Colin suggested Jenna retrieve Trooper from Gram's place and the four of them go for a walk.

"May I ask, are you a veteran? I see you also have a thing for camo leashes," Jenna said.

"Yeah, I was in the marines. Got out in '17. Where did you serve?"

And with that question, Jenna felt a rush of hope. Her time overseas had driven home how important it was to trust your instincts, and her instincts told her she could trust Colin.

"I said Trooper was having difficulty adjusting to this quiet life, but in truth I'm just as insecure as she is."

"I know it can be a hard road because I lived it, am still living it. I took advantage of a support group offered at the VA up in Wilmington."

"So, you're from around here?"

"I'm an attorney in Wilmington, but don't hold that against me," Colin said with a grin. "Guinness and I will be here another week and I speak for both of us when I say we'd love to hang out with you and Trooper until we go. Nothing too pushy; you set the pace."

"We would like that, too. Tomorrow at the beach?"

It was a mild day for the middle of January. Jenna and Trooper hopped out of the car and entered the unleashed-dog park. Trooper scoped out the enclosure, checking to see if her good buddy was among the group running around.

"They should be here soon, Troop."

A car door closed, and the gate opened. Trooper made a beeline for Guinness. Colin and Jenna kissed. They held hands as they watched the joyous romping of their dogs.

"I'm so grateful you make the trip down here each weekend. Thank you for that," Jenna said, as she leaned into Colin.

"It's good to see you getting stronger week to week." He kissed the top of her head. "I think back to the day the two of you were sitting in the sand trying to summon your courage."

"I thought I was saving Trooper." Jenna shook her head and smiled, as she watched the canine antics. "But actually, that girl saved me."

When Chris Jacobsen first heard the theme for this book she thought she would draw on her experience from her current position working for two veterinarians. However, she soon decided to focus on the other kind of vets, those with PTSD, one of whom she has been in a relationship with for over twenty years.

Chris has been grateful for the companionship of three dogs and ten cats over the years; the most recent feline, Nala, being a necessary adoption when her daughter married into a family with cat allergies.

Three of Chris's stories have been published in the Rehoboth Beach Reads anthologies, with the most recent being awarded third place in *Beach Dreams*.

This is Chris's sixth story to be published by Cat & Mouse Press.

Three Dog Night

by Kathaleen L. McCormick

Friday afternoon. Anticipation. The Kelly parents had managed to purchase a cottage in Ocean View, Delaware. Bridget Kelly called it her "biggest carrot."

"Kevin," she said to her husband, "this will bring our kids to us. With them come the grands. We won't have to grovel for their time; they will all come to the beach." And then she smiled her smug smile.

"You're right." Kevin got off the porch swing. "It will be wonderful having them all here for Memorial Day weekend. It will be the first of many happy family times."

Bridget closed her can of hot-pink paint and looked at the impressive mermaid she had painted on the shed, now tiki bar. Perfect. The kids will never want to leave this little paradise.

Patrick, son number one, was the first to arrive. He bounded into the house with his eight-year-old twins squealing and laughing behind. Cecelia and Nelia raced through the house and up the stairs. As Patrick put a case of Corona on ice in a cooler on the porch, he heard a piping voice.

"I get the top bunk!"

"Where is Meghan?" asked Bridget.

"She's coming," said Patrick. "She had to get the surprise out of the back of the car and walk it."

"It?"

"It. Here they are now."

At that, Patrick's wife, Meghan, came through the back door, pulling a pup on a leash.

"Meet our newest member, Lorhetta. She's a saluki," Patrick proclaimed.

"Lorhetta? What kind of dog's name is that?" asked Kevin.

Meghan explained that the pup's registered name was Lorhetta LaRue. The dog's father was Rhett the Blue and mother was Moira La Rue. Blend the names and you have Lorhetta La Rue.

"What ever happened to Princess, Rex, and Bingo for dog names?" asked Kevin.

"Princess, Rex, and Bingo are pound-dog names. Lorhetta cost twelve hundred dollars," Meghan retorted.

"Seriously?" Not waiting for an answer, Bridget sent the Kellys of Middletown, as she called her first son and his family, upstairs to unpack. "You and Meghan can take the blue room. The girls will be in the bunk room with their cousins."

With the Kellys of Middletown unpacking on the second floor, Bridget and Kevin watched the expensive saluki poop on the floor and then strut into the family room, where she made herself comfortable in Kevin's recliner. The matriarch and patriarch looked at each other with wide-eyed shock, then Bridget grounded the moment by grabbing paper towels, scooping the poop, and saying, "It's worth it. She's only a dog, and we will gain our children and grandchildren for a weekend like no other."

Later, she would wish she hadn't said those words. Often, what you say becomes what you get.

As the Kellys of Middletown settled in, Cecelia and Nelia making the bunk beds into a playhouse and the adults relaxing with Grotto pizza and Corona, the second son and his family arrived.

Ronan and his wife, Ann, were teachers in Denton, and their children, Mikey and Kerry, were in middle school. The Denton crew trooped in with more Corona, beach toys, and duffel bags. Following them, wagging his golden tail, was Bodi, the friendly Labrador retriever.

Bodi immediately eyed Lorhetta and pounced. Lorhetta responded with disdain. Bodi was not to be ignored. He leaped on her, knocking a lamp off a table. Mikey distracted the dogs by throwing a ball across the room.

As the lamp was being restored to the table, the door opened and in bounded Buddy, an Irish setter. In seconds, the dog had a pizza box in his mouth and was dragging it across the floor, attracting the interest of Bodi and the curiosity of Lorhetta.

"Buddy! Stop that." Summer, the third child of the Kellys, and her two girls, five-year-old Rose and four-year-old Daisy, entered the scene as chase led to chaos. "Mario," Summer announced, "will be down after his meeting. Enter late and make an entrance."

"Hold it," yelled Kevin, in his best coach voice. "Just hold it. Put your dogs in separate rooms … now."

But it was an effort that was a day late and a dollar short. Mikey, with ball in hand, had just opened the back door. He stepped into the yard, followed by the five girls and the three dogs. Lorhetta was first, with Bodi and Buddy in hot pursuit. Then, the dogs were gone. Gone like rabbits from a hat. Gone like Oreos from a cookie jar. Gone.

The household followed. Kevin went south, toward the park, with Kerry and Mikey in tow. Patrick headed across the field to the Assawoman Canal. Summer, tech savvy, perched on the deck at the house now dubbed the Mermaid House and worked on getting a locals-only site on Facebook so she could get the neighbors in on the search-and-rescue mission. Cecelia and Nelia cried. Rose and Daisy whistled and called and then were distracted by a stash of Popsicles they found in the refrigerator in the tiki bar.

Ronan and Ann jumped in their truck and headed toward Hocker's grocery store. There they saw a traffic jam at the entrance to Sunset Harbor and a blitz of brown and white and golden fur dashing into the Salt Pond development.

Bridget? She put the ham and the potato salad back into the refrigerator. No point in letting it sit out.

Joe, the artist neighbor yet to be met, worked frantically trying to capture the madcap scene for his beach art, which would later be sold at the Beach Plum emporium in Bethany Beach.

An hour later, the family straggled back. Kevin, Kerry, and Mikey, having gone from running to jogging to walking to dragging, were the first to reappear. Bridget handed Kevin a Corona as they heard Radio 94.7 predict a perfect weekend. Patrick and Meghan were next. Somehow, because Lorhetta La Rue had a hefty price tag, whereas Bodi and Buddy were pound dogs, Patrick felt entitled to be most aggrieved. Summer could not get onto the Wi-Fi and said she needed a glass of pinot grigio to help her think. Cecelia and Nelia had also discovered the comfort of Popsicles.

Thus was the scene when Ronan and Ann came rattling into the yard with three muddy dogs in the bed of the truck. Ronan, a coach like his Dad, was not thrilled. He had just had his prized blue truck detailed. The blue color perfectly matched his team's colors and the vanity license plate read, "Go Dawgs!"

"Hose them down and lock them up on the porch." Kevin sounded much like the football coach he had been, pre-retirement.

Ah! A brief peace, excluding the squealing from the bunk room, ensued. Certainly, these dogs did not know the fine art of the Irish exit, the way of quietly slipping away without fanfare. But if they had pulled an Irish exit, no one would have been searching, and possibly they would not have been found.

The Coronas certainly didn't hurt in soothing the stresses of the day, but the salty air was the best elixir. Bridget put the ham back on the table, and Meghan and Ann set the buffet and put out the sides. Summer snapped glow sticks.

This was what Bridget and Kevin had long dreamed of: a cottage by the sea, all of their offspring assembled, surf and sand, fishing and kite flying, sandcastles and seashells, bonfires and s'mores. Was this not the Delaware way? Bridget hummed "Wild Colonial Boy." Hearing her, Kevin sang, and all in earshot smiled. Yes, this was perfection.

It was at this idyllic moment that Summer's husband Mario arrived. He parked his black Lexus under the crape myrtle, grabbed his duffel bag and a case of Corona, and strode across the yard. Ann was the first to spot him as he approached the porch. He put his bag on the ground and reached for the door.

"Nooooo!" "Wild Colonial Boy" shifted to a chorus of warnings. "The dogs!" "Not that door!" "Mario, stop!"

But, yet again, it was a day late and a dollar short.

Bridget opened the door from the kitchen to the porch, hoping to grab the dogs. As she did, Bodi and Buddy rushed into the kitchen, and in a heartbeat the ham was gone. Lorhetta, that slick little canine Secretariat, skedaddled out the porch door, free again to run, to race like the waves, to sprint and dash and dance her flight of freedom and fancy. Like the ham, in only seconds, she was gone from sight. And in the chaos, Bodi and Buddy weaseled out the door as well.

This time, nerves were frayed like a seafaring rope. Corona had altered the blood chemistry. Hungry but well hydrated, the adults again took to the search. This time, however, it was dark as they wandered through the backyards of neighbors they had not yet met; curtains were pulled back and 9-1-1 calls were made.

"Stop where you are and put your hands in the air." Ocean View was known for its diligent police force.

"Let me explain," Patrick began.

"Hands up!"

"Look, I'm with the state police. I'm looking for my dog.

Let me reach for my wallet and I'll show you my ID." He squared his shoulders.

"State, huh? Never mind. Just call off the backyard search. The switchboard is lighting up."

Meanwhile, Bridget, the only adult who had not had an alcoholic beverage, took the keys to Ronan's truck, grabbed a package of hotdogs, and embarked on a broader search. *Think like a dog, think like a dog. Hmmmm. If I were a dog, I would follow the water.* She drove west, down Daisy Avenue and then back to the marina. A boat had just purred in and a big, red truck loomed in the lot.

It was there she found the bad boys. She called and Buddy came running and jumped in the truck, where she had placed the hotdogs. Bodi, though, was defiant. She enticed him with a hotdog, but he was resistant. Country music blared from the red truck. Finally, Bridget got close enough to grab Bodi's collar. She dragged; he pulled. The truck's lights came on and it pulled up next to her. Two young guys in caps got out.

"Is this your dog?" John Deere hat guy spit his snuff, and Bait and Tackle hat guy hooked his thumbs in his belt.

"My son's," Bridget huffed. Bodi's body language, however, said, "I have never seen this woman before in my life."

Bridget summoned all of her energy and pulled Bodi into Ronan's truck.

John Deere loomed over her. "We've had some dognappings around here. Black market." He spit his snuff again.

"And do I look like a black-market dognapper? I'm a grandmother!"

"You never know," said Bait and Tackle.

"No, I don't think either of you know much." Bridget's Irish was up, and her patience was down. Bodi and Buddy pressed their noses against the window. *Like dire wolves they are,* thought Bridget.

"Go Dawgs" pulled out of the marina parking lot and the red truck followed. In fact, it followed all the way to the cottage sporting a pink mermaid and only left when Ronan trotted to the truck, all smiles.

"Bodi, Buddy. Here, boys."

Once again, the dogs were put in lockdown. The ham was gone, but there was plenty of lunch meat, bread, and Corona.

"What about Lorhetta?" asked Kevin.

"She's chipped. If I don't get a call, it may be a loss well worth it." Oh, the fall from grace. So cavalier.

"Daddy!" Cecelia and Nelia clamored in unison.

"Let's get ready for bed and you can ask your guardian angels to bring her back." Meghan gathered her two children, and the other four followed like a conga line. "Up the wooden hill you go!"

Sunshine, like a sacrament bestowing solace, softly commenced Saturday morning. Kevin flipped pancakes, orange juice was the choice drink of the morning, and the newspaper was passed around in parts. Bodi and Buddy, having made it to the inner sanctum of kitchen, lurked under the kitchen table waiting for handouts of bacon and crumbs from Fractured Prune donuts and Bethany's Beach Break Bakrie and Café muffins. Hope sprang eternal when the phone call came.

"You have her? … Right … Can't thank you enough … super!" Patrick gave the address and put his phone back in his pocket. All eyes were on him. "Lorhetta has been visiting a family in Quillen's Point. She put on quite a damsel-dog-in-distress show. They fed her filet mignon."

"Why did you give this address? Shouldn't we go get her?" Meghan moved to get the car keys.

"Nooooo. They are sending her in an Uber. Anyone want a Bloody Mary?"

As the family waited to reunite with lavish Lorhetta, Rose and Kerry volunteered to walk Bodi and Buddy. Mikey was preparing to crab off the dock. The other children colored. Kevin and Bridget smiled at each other as they cleared the breakfast dishes. Radio 94.7 was playing a Three Dog Night song.

Summer came for a second cup of coffee. "I forgot to tell you," she said to her parents. "Aunt Jen called and said she is on her way. She said she'll sleep on the floor if she must. She's bringing her dog because the dog has had diarrhea for a few days, and she doesn't want to put her in the kennel."

Bridget's eyes widened. Before Kevin's jaw could drop, he caught a blur of brown fur in the window. He ran to the window and Bridget followed. What to his wondering eyes should appear, but Bodi and Buddy, dragging their leashes and dashing through the neighborhood. Rose and Kerry sprinted after them, but the distance between kept expanding.

Bridget, surprisingly calm, folded her dish towel and placed it neatly on the counter. "Irish exit?" She smiled over her shoulder, giving Kevin what could have been interpreted as a come-hither look.

Kevin took the keys to the Honda off the hook and, holding hands, the matriarch and patriarch strolled to their car and drove off.

Kathaleen L. McCormick is a retired educator. She has previously published professional research and articles and has had poetry and nonfiction published in local and international magazines and newspapers. Her first screenplay, *Brogues and Black Powder,* will be converted to novel format because, as she says, "Do you know how hard it is to market a screenplay when you live in Delaware?" Her inspiration for "Three Dog Night" was an actual three dog night! Kathy and her husband, Terry, live in Delaware, vacillating between Smyrna and Ocean View.

St. Peter's Magic Cat

by Terri Clifton

*I*t had been five nights since he'd left, her human, and he'd never even said goodbye. There hadn't even been a strange human coming by to refill her dish or let her into the sun porch. That had happened once, and for the first few days she was sure someone would come, until no one did.

Jade hopped from fence to window box and examined once more the emptiness inside the house. The flower box hadn't held any flowers in the months she'd lived here. It used to seem like a good place to nap; now it felt odd and sad. She wondered what to do.

She tried to remember what had come before, before he'd pulled her, shivering and wet, from under his car in the driveway. She couldn't. Sometimes when she slept, curled in the sun, she'd dream, or remember, or both, a warmth and a softness, others like her, and the smell of her mother. At least this time she was dry, and the days were warm.

Her person had named her Jade for the dark green of her eyes, and he had called her each day when setting out her food.

He'd let her inside when the coldest nights came and the world froze over, icy and white. Sometimes, he'd talk to her or pet her head as he passed by. Once, she'd sat next to him and purred herself to sleep. But he hadn't been home much, especially after spring arrived. And now that summer had come, he'd disappeared completely, with the boxes and the truck. She wondered if she was supposed to find him, and if so, where to look.

She stretched, trying to loosen the despair that wrapped itself around her body. Her eyes fell and refocused on the window's reflection. On the sidewalk behind her sat the big, yellow dog that wandered all over town and through everyone's lawn. He sniffed absolutely everything. And he chased cats.

Jade turned, ready to escape if it came to it, but feigned interest in grooming her paw. Safe in the window box, she smoothed the already sleek blackness and waited for him to move on. She'd seen him about, and in truth he was nicer than most dogs, but he had no respect for personal space. She'd once had to smack his impertinent nose. He'd never chased her because she had refused to run.

"Your person isn't coming back. I heard mine say it." Bo listened, even when he just couldn't obey. He'd been digging out and jumping fences forever, and everyone had just given up trying to change him. He always went back home. That's where his people lived.

He knew she wouldn't answer and didn't wait, breaking into a trot at the end of his street. Poor cat, he thought, heading for his dinner. She wasn't like the other ones, so sneaky and busy, and Bo never saw her about town, just on the steps or the garden wall. Bo didn't even think she chased the skinks that lived in the ivy. She'd never make it without a person, and it was a shame. She was one of the good ones. He could smell it.

Bo took his worry to sleep with him, twitching and whimpering, until his little girl, Gillian, reached over, scratched his head, and whispered his worries away.

The next morning, he decided to help. After a good breakfast, he bounded over the back fence.

Jade considered how best to catch the frog, lowering herself flat to the grass, tail twitching slightly, but knew it would dive into the koi pond before she could cross the open space of the neighbor's lawn. Still, she waited for a chance.

She couldn't believe the dog had discovered her here, crouched and peeking beneath the boxwood hedge, so tired and hungry she hadn't been aware of his intrusion until he was standing over her. The gate was open, and he looked pleased with himself. He opened his mouth and dropped half a cheeseburger next to her with a soft splat, then returned and sat by the gate. He was a dog, but it felt like kindness. It made her whiskers tingle uncomfortably. She didn't resist as long as she would have liked to before nibbling an edge. It wasn't bad and was far better than sinking her teeth into a frog. She left the bread, hoping he'd just think her finicky and not ungrateful. He'd slobbered on it, after all.

He'd waited by the road to give her the tour, show her the all the places the good stuff could be found. When she stopped chewing, he turned around and walked back. He looked at the bread left next to her.

"Not gonna eat that?" With no hesitation he gave it two chomps and a swallow. She didn't even know the basics. She'd left the ketchup and the pickle. Those were the best parts. He headed toward the gate, expecting her to follow. Which she did, but at a very respectable distance. Bo had never shown anyone his best spots, but he'd never known anyone that needed them before.

He went slowly, making a show of sniffing along the canal where boats came in, and more importantly, cleaned their catches. Past the *Overfalls* lightship and the ballpark, he skirted the tennis courts and waited for her under the pavilion before he rounded the shrubbery next to the inn. He trotted down the docks along the water, wove his way to the park, and halted under the trees. Jade had hopped atop the cannon facing the water. He barked a warning.

From Stripper Bites to the Rose and Crown he taught her where to find the best trash in town. When she leapt on a dumpster, he envied her some, but thought for the first time she might be OK, so he barked encouragement.

He looked longingly through the window of King's ice cream shop, and Jade used the bench to do the same. Bo knew he drooled a little when he gave his advice. He couldn't help it.

"The place to be on hot nights. Kids drip and drop. It's awesome." He stared another moment before moving on.

The bowl outside Biblion, the bookstore, had just been refilled. He hadn't meant to drink it all, but the water was cold and good. He looked down at the small cat with dust on her paws and felt guilty.

"I know a place. We just have to go in the back way. Too many people notice when I go over the gate."

The red brick of St. Peter's churchyard wall enclosed the square, and the high steeple towered far above the sidewalk as the dog and cat ran along. Jade realized it must look like she was chasing Bo, and that amused her.

Bo slowed down when he rounded the corner, and she followed him through a gap, into a small garden at the back of the old church. The shadows were long, as they wove along the path between the old graves. Bo stopped at a bubbling fountain that fell within the shadow of the new church. The water tumbled in tiers and was surrounded by flowers.

"Not a place for dogs to drink. But I'm sure it's OK for you."

He kept a look out until she stopped, then left her there to go back to his people.

That night, Jade slept under a bush, seeing no reason to go back to the empty house, and that's how she came to spend the entire summer living in St. Peter's square. There were dozens of crannies suitable for napping, and she liked living among the white headstones. She could walk the labyrinth late at night and use a paw to investigate the trinkets and coins left at its center.

She took advantage of all the things Bo had shown her and learned some things on her own. When Second Street became overrun with people on busy days, she'd headed for the park behind the Zwaanendael Museum, where she could nap in the herb garden or have a good roll in the catnip. On days she felt more sociable, she'd prance along the churchyard wall and let visitors stroke her fur or scratch her chin. Sometimes, they gave her treats. It wasn't a bad life. And she loved dropped ice cream. But summer never lasts forever.

When September came, the little resort town of Lewes slowed down, but not Bo. Gillian needed him to wait with her for the bus in the morning, and after that he'd run through the park, taking a shortcut to the elementary school, where he could watch her get safely off. He'd spend his day wandering the quieter streets, but would always be home in time to meet the afternoon bus.

First grade was harder than kindergarten, when she'd been home by lunch. She had homework that worried her, and she never seemed happy anymore, so he couldn't be happy either. On his saddest days, he'd sit outside the fence and wait for recess, just to catch a glimpse and know she was all right. He was so busy with his little girl that he almost forgot about Jade.

On the morning of the first hard frost, he was nosing around the historical society grounds when he noticed leaves falling. The wind picked up throughout the day and carried the leaves. They tumbled and skittered along the streets, some getting caught up and tossed high, only to float down again. When he passed the gate of the labyrinth, he saw Jade scampering and chasing the leaves about. She didn't see him as he paused in the shadow of Ryves Holt House to watch. She looked happy, so he didn't want to bother her with warnings of the cold to come.

That night, the rising wind brought a storm front. Wind and thunder rattled the house, and Bo's little girl was restless. A bad dream made her cry out, and her Mom came to sit on the bed until she felt safe again. Bo listened to the rain beating against the shingles and worried about the tiny cat. Alone. Probably cold. Maybe wet. There were only so many ways a dog could help.

He knew what he must do, and it would come with a heavy price. Bo was a good boy. He knew it and so did everyone else. That's why he dreaded the look on the Mom's face.

"Bad dog! Bad, Bo!" She shook the remnants of the stuffed toy at him, and he was ashamed. "Tonight is trick or treat and look what you've done."

Bo listened as she made call after call to stores and friends, trying to find another stuffed black cat. Between each negative response she scolded him again until he doubted himself and started to think he was a bad boy after all.

"Gilly is going to be so upset!"

He hated that thought. He didn't want to ever hurt Gilly. He hoped he wasn't ruining everything.

The rain and wind lasted for days, and Jade had run out of dry places, so she was pleased when Halloween morning the sun rose bright and strong. She stretched on the walkway, absorbed the heat, and waited for her world to dry. That's when she spotted Bo.

He'd seemed nervous asking the favor, and she was nervous about agreeing, but she saw his sad eyes and remembered how he had helped her when no one else had. That was why she was waiting where he asked, next to the pumpkins on the bookstore steps, just at dark.

Jade saw Gillian, dressed as a miniature witch, running toward her. Jade rubbed her dark head along the hem of the costume and purred. Gillian laughed and petted her, and Jade glanced at Bo, who still looked anxious. When the trick or treaters moved on, Jade followed, staying right next to the little girl, the perfect witch's cat. They stopped at each doorway, listened to people tell them how adorable they were, and watched Gillian's treat bag bulge. But Bo still looked nervous.

By the time they circled back to Bo and Gillian's house, Jade realized he looked scared. He walked so slowly that Gillian had to call him to catch up.

Bo knew this was it. In a few moments either everything would work out or he would be a failure and a bad dog forever.

Gillian's mom sat in the rocking chair on the porch as the three proceeded up the walk. She stared at Jade as her daughter approached.

"It's magic, Mommy. My stuffed cat got lost, but Bo found her, and she's turned real—look! She and Bo are already friends."

Bo saw many thoughts pass across the woman's face. She looked at Bo, who knew the lost toy was in the bottom of the trash.

"Let's go inside, Magic." Gillian turned the front doorknob. Warm light spilled onto the boards of the porch, as if inviting them in.

Bo held his breath.

Jade crossed the threshold into her new life, answering to her new name, and following Gillian into the house.

Behind her, the mother whispered to Bo. "I don't how you did this … but you're a good boy, aren't you?"

With a wag and a woof, Bo bounded after his little girl and her magical cat.

Terri Clifton was awarded an Emerging Professional Fellowship in Fiction Literature by the Delaware Division of the Arts. She is the author of a memoir, *A Random Soldier*, and her short stories and poetry have been published in more than a dozen anthologies. She makes her home on a historic farm in Sussex County, at the edge of the Delaware Bay, with her husband, Richard, an internationally known wildlife artist. One of her favorite writing spots is a bench in St. Peter's churchyard in Lewes. Her best dog friend, Finn, helped inspire this story.

Running with Joey

by Sherri Wright

When Joey sees me putting on my running shoes, he wags his wispy, black tail, stares with earnest, brown eyes and waits. For three months he chewed up shoes and chairs, tore through the house, and flopped his sloppy chew toys into my lap every time I sat down to read the newspaper. To use up his energy, I started taking him running.

My arthritic hands mold and fold onto his leash, and I hang on and try to steer at a pace faster than any race I've run. At the bridge I yell "stop" and plant my feet. I catch my breath.

Through years of running, I've lingered on this bridge to search for red-eared turtles, giant carp, and occasionally, the enormous snapper with beady eyes and a pink snout. I've watched mallard babies grow from fluff balls into iridescent feathered creatures. Herons and bald eagles perch in the crowns of these trees.

Joey lurches left, yanking me off the bridge after a squirrel. So fast! So strong! What kind of dog is this skinny puppy we adopted from the shelter last June? And why did his first mother abandon her beautiful, black baby with his white-cross chest and one white paw?

With both hands I force him back to the path to lure him the last quarter mile to the ocean. Joey tugs me onto the beach until the fragrance of a fish or a sand crab turns him in a circle. He digs. He tunnels. He spews wet sand into my face, my shirt, my legs, my old blue shoes.

I wonder how I will ever teach Joey—to slow down, to watch turtles under the bridge and birds in the trees, to taste salty air, to listen to the pulse of the surf, and to behold a red-orange sun as it rises out of the sea. To run my run. To be my child. To lead me and these old blue running shoes back home.

Sherri Wright is a member of the Rehoboth Beach Writers Guild and the Key West Poetry Guild. She runs, practices yoga, and volunteers at a center for homeless, all of which figure into her writing. Her work has been published in *Clementine, Panoply, Creative Nonfiction, Rat's Ass Review, District Lines Volume IV, Mojave River Review, Decimos-We Say, Prairie Schooner,* and *Delaware Beach Life.* Her dog Joey, a rescue who just turned three, still runs fast but will slow his pace slightly for a gecko or a rooster.

The Private Diary of Pippi, a Royal Cairn Terrier

by Carolyn Fogerty

*L*et me introduce myself. I'm Pippi. I live in a small house—similar to a prison—with only a half-acre, fenced in, to stretch my legs. I get walked two or three times a day, but am only fed twice daily, plus any tidbits I can scavenge by begging. So, you can see I'm really suffering. The world needs to know this.

Given my royal heritage, this situation is way below my standards. If you want my credentials, I'll be glad to dig them up for you. (Heh, heh, doggie joke.) I belong in a castle in Scotland, but the luck of the draw landed me here. Oh, don't get me wrong; the living quarters are clean, and Mom and Dad are decent folks who treat me well, considering they're humans and don't seem terribly bright at times.

But to show you what I'm up against, I submit this summary of a typical week:

Monday

Monday starts out as a perfectly normal day in Lewes. It

isn't New York, but it's all I've got. Anyway, it's a cute town with lots of interesting things to see and sniff. As we take our usual stroll, I can tell Dad hopes I don't embarrass him. Truth to tell, I'm hoping he doesn't embarrass me.

Well, hello. Look at that handsome boxer loping toward us. We greet each other, nose to nose in formal fashion (I'm not *that* kind of girl) and move on.

Dad and I walk to St. Peter's Cemetery, where he reads headstones and I find a nice patio to rest my paws on. Dad says I've been so well behaved he's considering a treat for us. We head toward King's Ice Cream, whereupon he buys himself a double-decker cone. I get a few measly licks before he inhales the rest in one swoop. *Typical.*

We return home for a little refreshment and a morning snooze when, before you can say "jackrabbit," I'm being hustled into the car for some unknown destination. Well, it all becomes clear when I hear Dad say we're going for my annual checkup, and I having no say in the matter.

To be fair, the vet is a swell person and so are the assistants. But what they do to you is hardly printable. Just because I'd been going bumpety-on-my-rumpety, they squeeze and poke me in very private places and then jab me with needles. Oh, the humiliation! But the last straw is when I hear the ol' Doc say to my human that I need to lose weight. I'll admit I do need to trim down a bit, but hey, have you looked at my human parents lately? Not exactly svelte. The ultimatum: cut out the rib eyes and all the other goodies a girl has come to love. Hopefully that regimen won't last more than a week. We pooches have that stare down to perfection, so the humans can't resist us.

Tuesday

I can tell right off this is not going to be what people call a red-letter day for me. From the furtive whispering between the resident neatniks (i.e. Mom and Dad, who forget that I have keen hearing), I know that words like "dirty" and "scruffy" can only mean one thing—a bath. Dad does the honors, which is an experience beyond belief. He waits until Mom leaves the house because she tends to freak out when he drops hair clippings, slops water all over, and drenches the mat.

The moment the coast is clear, he brings out the tools of torture: nail clippers and scissors. During this process, I bare my teeth every so often, just to keep him in line. Truth be told, he doesn't really hurt me, plus I'm not into violence, sweet natured soul that I am.

After the bath, the hairdryer comes out. By now, we've pretty much reached the limits of our patience. But finally, we're done. Dad steps back to admire his handiwork, while I grab the proffered treat and run to a safe place. Grudgingly, I admit I look and smell pretty good, but don't tell Dad I said so, or he'll make this bath thing a weekly event.

Next thing I know, there's much activity afoot—bags packed, car loaded, house locked, and Dad, Mom, and I are off to parts unknown (to me, that is). After several hours, a few pit stops, and lots of miles, we arrive at my cousin Sandy's house, tired but in one piece, no thanks to the scary human drivers, including Mom and Dad, who drive like maniacs.

I smell food. *Yum.* Once all the obligatory niceties are dispensed with, I decide to check out cuz's doggy dish. Sandy's a border collie—or maybe a bearded collie—and they feed him a lot. Yup, his dish is filled to the brim. *Slurp.* Yeah, it's good. Well, Sandy doesn't raise a paw, but my human uncle isn't too pleased,

When the humans gather at their trough, Sandy and I take up positions next to our dads (the moms are onto us) and wait for morsels to drop or be given on the sly. But before long, I'm being hustled back into the car for the ride home.

Wednesday

Today is one of Mom's exercise days, a study in futility. You gotta promise not to tell her I'm writing this; the poor soul has had enough humiliation trying on clothes recently. Here is my dog's-eye view of this spectacle.

I get alerted when I hear grunts and groans echoing throughout the house, clear to the padded cell where I've been trying to take my nap. But this show is worth the interruption. First, her legs go up, then *whomp* down again, then up, then *whomp*. It hurts just to watch. Next, she gets on all fours and tries to swing her leg sideways but falls over. She tries again, fails, and moves on. Now standing, she leans against the wall and stretches her legs, one at a time, and I'm sure I hear bones crunching (or maybe it's the wall cracking). Oh, brother, this is torture to watch. I hope she isn't too crippled to get our steaks on the grill for dinner tonight.

With good intentions, Dad takes me to the Lewes Un-leashed Dog Park. Old Dad can sure find some neat places for humans to meet and canines to sniff. The variety you see is astounding: small, large, fat, thin, ugly, handsome, friendly, testy—and that's just the people. It's a great feel-ing to stand still and be admired by the young pups. Being a matron exuding experience does have its advantages. It's also a good lesson in self-restraint if confronted by dudes the size of giants. They come lumbering up, trying to eyeball me. Fortunately, all are friendly—well, almost all. A few humans tend to get a might hysterical if they see any dog off the leash. You know the routine: "Is your dog friendly? Will he bite? Come here, no sniffing!" Oh, brother. These humans don't need a dog; they need a parakeet.

Thursday

It's early morning, and I'm writing this on a tree stump in the "back forty" (so to speak), our vast half acre of land. The dearth of flowers is pathetic. Mom's idea of a garden is a couple of trees and a bush or two scattered around. Yet she had the nerve to call the Chamber of Commerce to have our yard put on the Lewes Garden Tour. The woman is a fruitcake, I tell you.

It's inspiring to see wildlife coming and going, the four-legged and two-legged ones. The critters keep me busy chasing, but never catching. A calico cat saunters by, but I promised not to chase cats anymore. Dad said I wouldn't know what to do if I did nail one. Insulting. My breed is from a long line of ratters. See that rabbit? Whoa, he's a big one. Uh-oh, too late; he's gone. Toads have set up housekeeping under the porch, and squirrels come sniffing, but I chase them away. Rabbits get into the chase, and then we all go for a rest until the next round.

Uh-oh, here comes a formidable-looking animal. On closer view, I see it's only Dad. No one bothers with him. He's trying to decide if he should mow the lawn. Why? It will just grow again.

Dad and I go off to the schoolyard for a ball game (yay) on the pretext of getting some exercise. Lordie knows, if we each lost twenty pounds, who could tell? Anyway, after we arrive, he sits on a bench (some workout) and starts tossing out a few tennis balls whilst his doggy servant—that would be me—chases and retrieves them. After fifteen minutes of doing this, I'm thinking, *look who's doing all the work here.* Enough is enough; I'm onto his tricks. So, I hatch a plan, and that's to do a sit-down on his next volley of balls, which always end up far afield. Dad whistles for me to come back, but I'm hard of hearing, you know (heh, heh). He calls again, but I stick to the plan. Finally, he's forced to actually get up and walk a few yards. I'm all innocence, wagging my tail, smiling, and giving him that universal wide-eyed look we doggies have perfected. He melts, pats my head, picks up the balls, and we head home. I have visions of a tasty biscuit and a bowl of cool water to wash it down.

Friday

We're off to view the world of sand crabs and bikinis. Pale tourists are starting to make their debut, dragging beach bags, chairs, umbrellas, and kids. Every morning, they arrive early and circle around the parking lot in their cars to see if the ocean is still there. It is.

We commandeer a bench, Dad hoisting me up onto his skinny lap, and the three of us (yes, Mom came, too) watch humanity waddle by. What a show! The short shorts, the long shorts, the shorts with white socks and sandals, and the flashing sneakers. Some youngsters rush up to pat and admire me. "Oh, she's so cute!" (They're talking about me, Mom, sorry.) Wait, there's more.

You know the canard, "Guns don't kill people; people kill people"? Whoa, there's a scary thought. So, just to be fair, here's a real good one to chew on (heh, heh): "Doggies don't pollute; people do." We love Mother Earth, even if some of us do a bit of digging now and then—you know, to aerate the soil. But we don't drop cigarette butts or toss trash out car windows. Never. But people don't understand how trash can harm us all, like how balloons and pieces of plastic can lodge in small throats.

I spot a handsome setter therapy dog, proud in his red vest and harness. Not bad, but he'll get no encouragement from me. I'm a dignified matron, you know. Still, fun to look, as Dad always says when he ogles those bikinis (until Mom gives him a swat).

Well, I thought I'd heard everything until I learned there is a day in June called "Take Your Pet to Work Day." I'm thinking, are they kidding? My humans don't even go to work, and the little they do around the house is pathetic. He mows a few blades of grass and calls it a day. She washes a couple of dishes and takes a nap. Anyway, my neighbor buddy, Moby, a rather heavyset bulldog that snorts and belches a lot, was taken to his master's workplace to be shown off. *Whatever.* After he returned home, he informed me that the whole thing was a disaster. All the pets did was sniff out stashed lunch bags and get into wastebaskets. One cutie peed on the boss's leg, and one (I suspect Moby) let some of his wind go free. The pets were removed from the premises and all vowed to never step foot or paw in a workplace again.

Saturday

Today's the garage sale, the day when the collectors of America (um, OK, Sussex County) gather at the "Shrine of Detritus." Translation: when our neighbors put a motley collection of goods, in their ninth life, on display, hoping to give them a new home. We puppies fear for our lives, so we observe this maniacal ritual from afar.

A question: Why are they called "garage sales"? Are the garages for sale? And why bother posting "no early birds"? By six a.m. the hunt is on. Cars are cruising, with hunters waiting to pounce. Many are dealers who scan the displays, but generally find no treasures and leave. Next come the late risers, looking for bargains (like discounts on twenty-five-cent items). The nerve. Last, the laggards arrive, thinking everyone is tired by now and will just give it all away to be rid of the stuff. *Uh-huh.*

My Mom and Dad love to recycle. Dad recycles his clothes. For the first few years, a pair of pants are Sunday-go-to-meeting pants; then, they become go-to-grocery-store pants; a couple years later, they serve as work-in-the-yard pants; and finally (unbelievable), the pants are cut off to become shorts. As for Mom's clothes (in case you're wondering), she hoards them because she says they may fit her someday. *Dreamer.*

All goes well at our digs until some folks start eyeballing my things—familiar old collars, a nicely broken-in bed, a couple of well-worn blankies, and a five-year-old, half-chewed bone. So, from where I'm hiding, I come out and show some teeth, 'cause this is gettin' personal. If those humans don't get their paws off my treasures, Judge Judy will be hearing from me. We doggies have rights.

Sunday

Check it out, you folks looking for a pet. There are lots of lonely animals out there wishing for a loving home. And they don't have to be pedigreed to be worthy and beautiful. That old mutt down the street is my best friend; you don't need papers to have character. Stop by and see for yourself what delightful animals the shelters have. You won't regret it; I promise.

Well, it's getting pretty close to dinnertime, but no activity—none—in the culinary department. That's because it's clean-out-the-refrigerator day. Mom is doing her ritual, i.e. pulling out everything from the fridge, dead or alive, and placing it ceremoniously on the kitchen counter. A couple of dry summer squash, an unrecognizable vegetable, a custard cup of mac and cheese (which really needs help), and two wrinkled hotdogs (buns missing). Mom calls this her buffet. *Yuck.* She's kidding, right? No, she's not.

Witness the *coup de théâtre*: Two large bottles of wine are brought out, the lights dimmed, and some candles placed for atmosphere. After announcing "dinner" is served, Mom and Dad promptly get into the libations, pass crackers and cheese, and very soon, there are smiles all around. Go figure.

Well, that's about it for the week. Let me leave you with these words of wisdom:

A good belly rub is always appreciated.

A juicy rib eye is worth its weight in doggy biscuits.

Even if we seem brave, a warm lap is welcome during a

thunderstorm.

When we get sick, we count on you to help.

Don't even try to sneak out of the house without us, thinking we won't know—we *always* know.

When we hear those car keys jingle, we are up and ready.

If you're not home at your usual time, we worry.

We'd never betray your trust. You know those secrets you share with us? They're still secrets.

Thanks for hearing me out.

– *Pippi*

Carolyn Fogerty is a retired musician who studied at the Oberlin Conservatory, where she also minored in English and ultimately became a piano teacher and an organist. In 1994, she and her husband, Ron, moved from Pennsylvania to Lewes, Delaware, after their children were grown and her husband retired. She continued to serve as a church organist, but her love of literature also inspired her to write tales of the antics of their cairn terrier, Pippi. Her dream was to share these tales in a weekly local newspaper, but the editor showed no interest. Consequently, those tales were shared with her children and then stored in a folder until she heard about the *Sandy Paws* project. That's when Pippi came out again to play in "The Private Diary of Pippi." If only her husband had lived longer so he could enjoy reminiscing about their lives with cairn terriers.

For the Love of Dave

by Kathy Maas

He was in the middle of a long line of barking, howling, and growling canines in cages at a shelter forty miles inland from The Salt Pond in Bethany Beach, Delaware. Most of the dogs were pit bulls. He was of indeterminate breed, smallish and trembling, and he piddled a little as the young couple walked by.

Elliott and Ella walked down the entire aisle out of politeness to the kennel attendant, but both knew they'd be circling back. They knelt at the cage, and Ella stuck her fingers through the metal lattice.

"Hey, little guy," she said, though the dog may not have heard due to the harsh, echoing clamor. He licked her fingers and then shrunk back, head down and one leg bent at the forearm. He looked as though he was politely genuflecting, and that sealed the deal.

The drive home seemed to take forever. The dog stood shivering on the floor in the back of the car the entire time. Elliott didn't know if he should pet him or hold him. He decided to let the dog be.

Once in the house, Elliott unhooked the leash from the dog's collar. The man and woman sat on the floor in the living room. The dog eventually sat but didn't move from the spot where they'd taken his leash off.

"Hmm," Ella said. "He doesn't really look like an Apollo."

"Yeah," the man agreed. "Or a Diesel." He took the baggie, one that he'd packed for the trip, out of his pocket and offered the dog a treat. "Come 'ere, bud. I have a goodie for you." The dog's nose twitched almost imperceptibly, but he remained still except for the trembling. "He looks like a ... Dave."

"Dave!" Ella laughed. "Where did you get that?" She noticed the dog avoided her gaze whenever she tried to make eye contact. After a while, she said, "But, yeah, Dave does kind of fit."

And that was that.

After two weeks, Dave's shivering subsided, except for an occasional bout of nervousness brought on by the heavy-duty partiers who lived next door.

It took a bit longer for him to acclimate to the rhythms and flow of life on Oyster Shell Cove. Elliott, who was sometimes known as Wax Man, had a deep and rather loud voice, and Dave was slow to warm up to him.

Weekdays, when only Elliott was home, Dave restlessly roamed the house, looking for things to chew. He spent a lot of time staring out the sliding glass doors of the sunroom, barking at people, cars, and little creatures darting about. He steered clear of Elliott, who was always swinging his long, jangly limbs on and off the sofa and stumbling around the kitchen in the morning. His sharp yelps and exclamations when watching the television bothered Dave.

When Ella returned home each day, Dave would work himself into a frenzy, twisting and barking and jumping on Ella's scrubs, eagerly inhaling the day's trace accumulation of antiseptic, blood, and other substances. He would then follow her around for the rest of the day, up and down stairs, into the yard and such, and lie by her side of the bed at night.

By summer, though, Dave had gotten used to Elliott.

Ella never failed to fill his food bowl with multicolored bits ("nutrient dense and protein packed!"), but Elliott would offer him bits of whatever he was eating when he worked at the computer. Things with sausage and pepperoni rarely hit the floor, no matter how carelessly they were tossed. Dave really enjoyed morning walks with Ella, as many dogs lived in the neighborhood, but riding on Elliott's surfboard was wildly thrilling.

"Let's go, Davey-O!" Elliott would shout, and Dave would race to the front door, then to the car, and sit regally until Elliott opened the door. No matter how hot it was, Elliott would roll down the window so Dave could stick his nose out and inhale the intoxicating smells of a beach town in season.

At first, they went to Indian River Bay, with its predictable, teeny waves. Whether it was because of his short legs or his perfectly situated center of gravity—or because he was just a highly athletic dog—he quickly became comfortable balancing on a surfboard.

After a few weeks, Elliott took him oceanside, north of Campbell Place. To build Dave's confidence and skill, they only went out when the water was calm. Dave had trouble getting used to the life jacket Elliott bought for him. He tried to shake the vest off, then chew it apart, but was unsuccessful. For Elliott, it was convenient; the handle on the back allowed him to grab Dave out of the water and onto the board in one swift motion.

Everyone who watched the twosome agreed it was a beautiful sight. Man and dog, silhouetted against the sky, the sunlight making bouncy ribbons through the waves. It took practice and more than a few spills, but Dave was always eager to try again.

When the weather turned cooler, the threesome went on long walks. Their favorite hiking spot was in the woodsy calm of Fresh Pond Trail Head. El&El, as they called themselves, would take turns holding the leash and were good about picking up Dave's deposits, even when no one was watching. Dave would let loose on these trips, trotting jauntily here and there to sniff this and that. He'd sometimes strain on the leash, then turn back to look at them. They both thought it looked like he was smiling.

Winter was mild that first year. Sometimes El&El took Dave for romps and ball fetching on the beach. Dave rushed along the hard sand, leaping quickly and gracefully, leaving tiny footprints to be erased by the next long swash. At some point during each outing he'd dash into the surf, only to yip and halt in surprise at the icy chill.

The town swelled as the weather grew hotter. By the end of June, Dave became quite skilled at surfing solo, with Elliott simply giving a little push at the beginning of the ride. Dave would sometimes do the little bowing motion that he did in the kennel, endearing him to any passersby.

Dave was becoming a local celebrity. People would jokingly ask for his autograph or shout, "Hang twenty!" (even though it would be impossible to hang all four feet off the edge, not to mention that Dave only had 16 toes). One nice lady even gave Dave a neon-green doggie T-shirt with the words "Eddie Would Go" across the back, a nod to Hawaiian surfer Eddie Aikau, known for taking on waves others wouldn't.

"Wax Man and little dude!" friends would call out. "Can I get a selfie with you guys?" Lots of regulars knew Elliott through his part-time gig at Bethany Surf Shop. Some were loyal to the line of surf waxes he'd developed. A few even knew him from his longform essays in *Sports Illustrated*, though he'd only had a few pieces published thus far.

But Dave and Elliott together were newsworthy. They'd already been interviewed by several reporters and photographers in the region. A local business offered to build a float featuring them for the town's Fourth of July parade.

Kids loved Dave. He was gentle with them. He wasn't one to bark and jump up in excitement (that was reserved for Ella). Lots of folks wanted to pet him, which he accepted but didn't seek out, and he wasn't fickle like some dogs. Dave was just … cool.

On a brilliantly sunny day in mid-July, a middle-aged woman approached Elliott at the ocean's edge. "My son is fascinated by you and your pup. We've been watching you for a few weeks now." She hesitated. "Do you think … is there any way my son could ride on the surfboard with him?"

Elliott looked over at their beach set-up. A boy about eight was zooming a toy truck back and forth over the sand, making engine noises. "Um, well … I guess we could try it," said

Elliott. "We've never done anything like that before. Maybe if he just holds the back of the board gently so Dave—my dog—can keep his balance."

"Oh," the lady interjected quickly, "I don't know if that's possible. My son has some challenges. He doesn't necessarily follow directions."

Elliott thought a moment and looked at the boy again. He was still racing the car back and forth. "RRRrrrRRrrr!" Elliott remembered those noises; he'd done that as a tyke, playing with his Hot Wheels cars.

"Let's give it a go," he told the boy's mom. "Does he know how to swim?"

"Yep. And he knows how to boogie board. He was quite good at it, but there was an accident two years ago, and now he's afraid of a lot of things ..."

They coaxed the boy over to meet Dave. It took about ten minutes. Getting into the water did not happen that day, nor did it the next day.

A day came when Elliott was out surfing with Dave and saw mom and son on the beach. Elliott was shocked when he saw the boy simply walk down the beach and into the water without prompting from anyone. The boy shrieked and slapped his hand on the tumbled remains of a wave. Elliott guided the surfboard into the shallow water toward the child.

"Jesse!" His mom came running down the sand.

"Hold the board like this." Elliott indicated with his hands.

Jesse grabbed the board. He had a surprisingly strong grip. The woman got behind him and guided his hands into the position Elliott suggested. Elliott held Dave by his lifejacket to steady him.

It was an exhilarating day.

Hours later, Elliott and Dave arrived home. Both were exhausted. Elliott fell onto the bed, while Dave went around to Ella's side and flopped on the floor. They were asleep within a minute.

The next morning, Elliott was writing an essay about a major league baseball player he'd interviewed who had a PhD in astrophysics. The guy was fascinating, but Elliott's mind kept wandering to the day before. He'd never had much patience and found that Jesse required a lot of it, yet he hadn't even noticed at the time. And Dave's calmness seemed to lessen the boy's unruly yanks on the board. Plus, it turned out that Jesse could talk, though he was not a conversationalist.

Elliott was also taken aback by a strong feeling of tenderness toward the kid. Where the heck did that come from? He and Ella had agreed years ago that they didn't want offspring. In fact, they sometimes fell on the sofa laughing with relief after friends with children left their house. Conversations about the minutiae of little Trevor's T-ball tantrum or Olivia's wardrobe antics left them straining for how to reply. Could it have been that they just didn't get to know those kids? Then again, he didn't know Jesse well, either.

Elliott told Ella about it over dinner that night. It was nothing he could pinpoint, exactly, but he felt a bit let down afterward. Perhaps once Ella met the boy, she'd feel it, too. Elliott puzzled over it all throughout the week.

Surfing with Jesse became a regular activity. Jesse's mom

would tell Elliott their schedule, and if Jesse couldn't make it because of a doctor's appointment, which apparently wiped him out, Elliott found himself looking forward to their next meet-up.

In mid-August, Wax Man and little dude took on another protégé. A gleeful girl playing at the water's edge was entranced by them. She'd waved often, though they were unable to wave back while surfing. On the third day of this, Elliott approached the girl's parents and offered a ride, which turned into almost two weeks of lessons and delight until the family's vacation ended. Elliott had never known a person with Down syndrome, and if anyone had asked his thoughts on the experience, he—a wordsmith—would not have been able to verbalize it.

That winter, El&El had fewer conversations and spent less time lounging in the living room together checking their cell phones. Dave padded from one to the other, often in separate rooms. Ella would scratch his head for a while, then Elliott would play fetch with him. Eventually, Dave would nap at the foot of one, then the other. They also spent less time hiking in the woods. Ella still walked him through the neighborhood but now spent more time talking with neighbors and less time striding purposefully to keep up with Dave. He'd tug the leash, eager to move on, and when she didn't take the hint, he'd circle her legs so she'd have to untangle herself.

By summer, El&El had become El and El. Elliott moved into a townhouse owned and inhabited by a coworker from the surf shop. Ella remained in the house at The Salt Pond. They agreed that Elliott would have primary care of Dave, as he was able to be home more often and Ella's shifts were erratic. Ella would take care of Dave whenever Elliott was out of town.

Both realized that while they were deeply grieving over their parting, Dave was devastated as well. They made sure to shower him with hugs and attention, brushing his hair frequently and letting him sleep on furniture, which Ella had never allowed in the past.

The surfing escapades continued for years. Sometimes Dave and Elliott received references from Children's Beach House in Lewes and Nemours/Alfred I. duPont Hospital for Children in Wilmington. Kids as old as seventeen and as young as three were able to experience the "squee!" of surfing with a wonder dog. The experience never lost its thrill for Dave or Elliott. Dave even learned a few tricks on the board, which delighted the audiences they'd developed along the shorelines.

A few years after the couple parted ways, Elliott remarried. By then, Ella's mom had moved into the spare bedroom at Oyster Shell Cove.

Each life shift was a time of adjustment for Dave. But the surfer dog was used to getting back on the board after taking a tumble. The birth and childhood of Elliott's twins provided Dave with endless amusement. And he was most agreeable to sleeping in "grandma's" lap, which he did more and more as the years went by.

Sixteen years after "not an Apollo" ("or a Diesel") was rescued from the cage at the shelter, El and El met one last time in the veterinarian's office, when they were told there was nothing that could be done. They held Dave gently, encircling him with their memories and tears. They kissed him and called him "Davey-O" and stroked his ears, agreeing that he'd had a great life, and they had indeed known the best love.

Kathy Maas is a resident of Delaware and incorporates her photography and art into her writing whenever possible. She is published in *Hint Fiction: An Anthology of Stories in 25 Words or Fewer* and is a past contributor to *Junior Baseball* magazine. She placed third in an essay contest on the Modern Era Baseball website, second in a national writing contest for her ten-thousand-word essay "Wild Boys," and was the 2018 grand prize winner in the Shield Healthcare Caregiver Essay Contest. The character of Dave was based on the family pet Tucker, who doesn't surf but is one seriously cool dog.

Meanderings with Maisie

by Mary Dolan

*Y*ou've heard it said that the gods laugh while we're making plans? Well there were belly laughs in heaven that day. My plan was to spend a month in historic Lewes, Delaware, house-sitting for a friend, her secluded home on a dead-end street providing the peace and quiet my inner curmudgeon yearned for. Her mother had insisted on keeping her grand dog for the month. Canine caretaking being well outside my comfort zone, this arrangement suited my plan perfectly.

Free at last from a lifetime of teaching creative writing to high school seniors, I anticipated enjoying the summer solitude with all the time in the world to edit short stories. Sadly, other writers' short stories. The business of living left little time to follow the dream of penning work of my own. Someday, I tell myself. Someday.

Armed with a portfolio of entries for a short story competition, I drove my twenty-two-year-old Subaru down Route 1, only to encounter a massive traffic backup on Route 9 in Lewes. Arriving later than I'd promised, I got out of the car just as a taxi pulled up to the picturesque house, front garden awash in a seasonal profusion of multicolored hydrangeas.

My friend emerged from the house, turned her luggage over to the driver, and told me she had to rush to make her plane. Everything was explained in a note on the coffee table, and she was sure I would have a wonderful month. A quick hug and then the cab made a U-turn and headed for the BWI airport.

I stopped on the wraparound porch and took a moment to lounge in a wicker rocker and count my blessings. How lucky was I to have the whole month to myself to explore this lovely old village, to edit at my leisure and not be obliged to speak to a solitary soul. This was my idea of paradise.

Another maxim to add to those laughing gods goes like this: If it sounds too good to be true, it probably is. You knew this was coming, right? As soon as you heard there was a note. It was not one to tell me where the tea bags were kept.

But I was blindsided.

I heard the soft bark first. Certainly, it was from next door. Grace's dog is with her mother. Of course Grace's dog is with her mother.

Time to read the note.

> *Dear Polly,*
>
> *Everything happened so fast, I didn't have time to give you all the details before I left, being more than a little frazzled, as you will understand. Late last night as I was driving Maisie to my mother's, she called from the ER. I'm afraid she sprained her ankle badly enough that she won't be walking for a few weeks, and it was too late to make other arrangements.*
>
> *You'll find my girl in the backyard. Don't worry, Pol. Maisie is sixteen years old, a bit arthritic, and*

very happy with two walks a day and nightly snuggle time. One of our favorite strolls is through downtown Lewes. Everybody in town knows her, and she stops for treats at all her favorite spots. By the time I come home, you will be friends with the whole village.

Kibble is under the sink; feeding instructions are alongside her bowl on the counter near the coffee maker. I'm sure it will be love at first sight between you.

Love, Grace

Goodbye vacation. It's time to face the music.

Stopping for a moment in the kitchen, I couldn't help being captivated by its old-world charm. A farmhouse table surrounded by four, mismatched, cushioned chairs, claimed the center of the small room. Glass-fronted cabinets displayed haphazard patterns in mugs, bowls, and plates. Thriving spider plants hung in macramé baskets at every window, while cherry-red geraniums bloomed in pots on the sills below. The only nod to modern living was the chrome espresso maker next to the pottery bowl that read *Maisie.*

Another bark roused me from my reverie, and I moved toward the screen door to the back porch. Opening it, I saw nothing but a wildly overgrown yard awash in tiger lilies and black-eyed susans and a stockade fence covered with the fragrant orange blossoms of trumpet vines.

Lost in the image of hunkering down in that garden, nose in a book, I felt rather than saw a black-and-white figure climb the steps and sit at my feet. She had a thick, wavy coat, a freckled face, long ears, and eerily expressive eyes.

"You must be Maisie," I said, then felt ridiculous for talking to a dog. You couldn't have told me then that by the end of the month she'd have turned my life on its head. Right then, she was simply Maisie, Grace's dog. I would feed and walk her in exchange for living in this lovely home. But there was no way I was about to be "friends with everyone in town." No way.

It was still early in the day. Maybe a walk into town would do us both good. Agreeing wholeheartedly with that decision, Maisie nose-nudged a leash hanging on the kitchen door. Hooking it to her collar, I followed her through the house, checked the lock on the door, and wandered down the street toward town. I knew of the Village Bakery from my own local farmers' market in nearby Maryland, and I was interested in seeing their actual store. But I soon figured out who was in control of this journey. I was at the other end of the leash. Maisie was captain of the ship and she was not in a race for the shore.

Grace's block featured some of the oldest homes in the village, and Maisie stopped at each of them and started up the walkway toward the porch. I held her back, especially when I spotted a figure sitting on one of the porches. She, on the other paw, was having none of it.

At one house, a woman I'd place in her eighties met us at the top step, reached into a small bowl near the railing, and handed Maisie a tiny biscuit. The scratching behind the ear at one end and wildly wagging tail at the other told me I was in the company of friends—the very last thing on earth I wanted.

As I tried without much success to pull Maisie along, the old woman smiled, seemingly approved my stewardship of Grace's dog, asked my name, said she was called Elizabeth, and asked whether I played bridge. My first mistake: I said yes.

Nearing the edge of downtown, on the corner of the main street, Maisie paused, then wandered toward the entrance to Buttercup, a restaurant with a cozy, glassed-in dining porch. As I attempted to pull her back—unsuccessfully, of course—I saw the hostess leave her post, pick up something from under the reservation desk, come down the stairs, and offer it to Maisie. Another biscuit. I don't have to tell you of the head scratching and tail wagging; you're getting the picture by now. But were you as surprised as I when the co-owner of Buttercup, Kathleen, invited me for a complimentary lunch on the porch and asked me to bring "the wee one" (in Irish-accented words) with me? It seems that Grace and Maisie are regulars at the eatery and friends with the entire staff.

My second mistake: I accepted, and soon my personal history was fodder for every server, busboy, and diner. Maisie daintily enjoyed snack offerings from everyone, along with the now-familiar head rubs, while I unpacked the luggage of my life, naively admitting I was a jigsaw puzzle fanatic, and let slip my cell number.

After lunch and a chorus of "see you soon," we continued our stroll toward the bakery. It was a two-minute walk along a shop-filled street, but meandering with Maisie transformed it into a twenty-minute garden tour. Shuffling along, every scent beckoned. Her keen nose sniffed each store's window box, some with spicy sage and thyme, many with marigolds and long trails of lantana. Our pace was perfect for deep breaths of air, blossomy with a smidge of salt, a precious interim for me to stop and smell the roses. The leash was loose and I followed her lead.

At the bakery, a customer on her way out held the door,

and Maisie pulled me inside as though it were home and I was her visitor. I was still full from our generous meal, but the smell of baking bread assaulted my senses and nothing would do but to ask for one of their still-warm baguettes. Ah, I thought, here I am an anonymous customer. My privacy won't be invaded. Nobody is going to ask if I play Scrabble. But as I was paying for the bread, a short woof was enough to alert the saleswoman that I was not alone. Coming around from behind the counter, she opened her arms, and Maisie pulled away from me and ran to her. Yes. Head rubs. Tail wags.

The woman introduced herself as Chloe. Already knowing that Grace was touring the Greek islands for the month and I was the friend from Maryland, she asked if I wanted to take Grace's place in their book club. The current book is short, she told me, and they won't meet until the end of the month, so I'd have plenty of time to read it and sort out my impressions. You know what came next. My third mistake.

I made the decision to circumvent the other side of the street and head back to Grace's. Maisie seemed tired but stayed alongside me, and we soon reached the welcome solitude of the old house; however, it was a bit less solitary than I had hoped. A note, addressed simply "To Polly" had been slipped under the screen door and I was more than a little reluctant to open it.

The handwriting was beautiful cursive, leading me to think it was from Elizabeth, the neighbor down the street. I'm sure she would never be caught texting. Unfolding the crisp, white vellum, I found an invitation to be a fourth at bridge on Tuesday nights while Grace was away. She said it went without saying that Maisie was expected to attend these events with me since she always came along.

Well, now I know the origin of the phrase "the best laid plans." Still, it was only one night a week. Surely my autonomy would not perish over a few hours of bridge. Why are you laughing? And why is my phone buzzing? I'd told everyone at home that I needed this month to work without interruption, and what few friends I have know better than to cross me.

But this text was from Kathleen at Buttercup, informing me that a few staff members would be over on Monday with a thousand-piece jigsaw puzzle. The subject was Edward Munch's painting, *The Scream,* a metaphor for my hijacked solitude. She said they always did the puzzles at Grace's so Maisie wouldn't be left alone, and not to worry about lunch. The restaurant was closed on Mondays, and they would raid the larder for all the food we needed. They'd be here around noon.

So, there went Monday afternoons along with Tuesday evenings. I'd control the rest of the time by taking Maisie to Cape Henlopen State Park for our outings, staying out of the socially hazardous downtown.

Preparing our dinner, I began to feel better about the coming month. I still had five full days each week to work on the edits and perhaps fuel my own creativity enough to come up with the first draft of a short story. Perhaps I overreacted to the two invitations. I didn't have to give away any more of myself than I chose to. Everything would be all right.

So why did I break out in a sweat when my phone buzzed again with a text from Chloe, the clerk at the Lewes Bakery? The book club. I'd completely forgotten. She said she'd gotten my number from Kathleen (it's a small town), and she had a copy of the book for me to pick up. I learned that the group met on the last Thursday of the month and, yes, without having to ask, was told that Maisie was welcome to attend.

Sunday morning, I awoke more rested than I had in years, surprised to find Maisie on a cushion at my feet, but more surprised that I wasn't annoyed to see her there. We padded down to the kitchen together, me to construct a latte in the espresso maker and warm some of yesterday's baguette, Maisie to survey her domain from the back garden.

After breakfast, we wandered toward town again to pick up the book from Chloe. A stop at Elizabeth's first, though, for a warm greeting, a doggie treat, and a reminder about Tuesday night—seven p.m., sharp. I found I was looking forward to it. I hadn't played bridge since I was president of the bridge club in college. Why, I wondered, and then continued on our walk.

Passing Buttercup, I was pleased to see such a large crowd on the porch for brunch. I told Maisie that next Sunday we would have brunch together and I could get to know her many friends better. It did not feel in the least bit off to be having a conversation with this dog. What was going on?

We picked up the book at the bakery, went back to Grace's for my car, and drove out to the beach. Dogs are not permitted during the summer season, so Maisie and I nestled above the dunes and breathed in the salty sea air while we listened to the garrulous gulls and relaxed into the rhythm of the incoming and outgoing waves. I think we both even dozed for a few minutes before heading home. That afternoon, I settled on a porch rocker and began reading the book, losing myself in the plot twists, as Maisie napped by my side.

On Monday at noon, the thousand-piece puzzle arrived

in the hands of three fellow addicts from Buttercup. We set it up on Grace's dining-room table, each of us taking a seat on our own side and began to sort the edge pieces. At one point, someone got up and rattled around in the kitchen, then reappeared with a tray of finger sandwiches and a restaurant specialty, raspberry iced tea.

Grace's collection of early jazz CDs provided soothing sounds from another room. Voices rose and fell between bursts of laughter and silence, everyone dedicated to their section of the puzzle. I realized it didn't matter whether we completed this challenge. The important thing—the essential thing—was our connection. No one was alone. Eight hands moved as one, two of them surprisingly mine, and more surprisingly, I felt happy.

After that Monday, I began to look forward to the next week's puzzle session and hoped my bridge skills were up to the game on Tuesday night. They were. I won more hands than I lost but, unlike in my college days, I didn't care either way. The joy was in playing the game and the amazing people I played with.

Every day, Maisie and I wandered the old, narrow streets of Lewes, stopping to chat with other dog walkers or for her to be admired by young and old alike. Elizabeth, Chloe, Kathleen, and the Buttercup crew accepted me into their fold purely because of Maisie. If I was OK with her, I was OK with them. Our Monday afternoons and Tuesday nights blended seamlessly into each other throughout the month. In between, I edited the short stories, but found my mind drifting to thoughts of the folks I'd met and the unseen people who beautify their own small corners of the world. Some I knew; some I'd create. But I was going to write about them all.

Suddenly, it was coming up to the last Thursday, the night of the book club meeting. Grace would be home on Saturday. And I would be going home.

Well, you can say "I told you so," and you would be right. This old curmudgeon never got her solitude. And the gods surely did laugh out loud at the plan, but now they are smiling.

Since coming home, I have completed the first draft of my novel. The setting is Lewes, and its characters are bridge-playing, jigsaw-puzzle-solving, and widely read townsfolk. Individuals who were woven into a family by an aging springer spaniel named Maisie, who stole my heart during one magical month that summer.

Mary Dolan never had an animal in her life until just before her fiftieth birthday. And he, Cappy, was a cat! But she says his is a story for another time. This one has been about Maisie, the sweet springer who shared a home with two mommies, two golden retriever brothers, and six cats. Both the curmudgeon and the pup were carved from whole cloth.

This is Mary's third story in Cat & Mouse Press anthologies. She came to fiction late, following careers in both public relations and photography. Her current challenge surrounds wrestling with the mystery genre, hoping to make her fourth Cat & Mouse Press appearance.

The Ginger

by Linda Chambers

*T*he ginger cat lived at the Village Mall in Chincoteague. What I mean is, she lived behind the mall, in the parking lot. That's where I met her.

It was mid-August. Having started my drive from Baltimore later than I'd intended and with traffic heavier than I expected, I made and remade numerous things-to-do lists in my head during the three hours plus.

I turned onto Rt. 175 for the final eighteen-mile push to the island, my list pretty much finalized. I'd do my grocery shopping the next morning at Island Foods Great Valu on Cleveland. I'd stop at Church Street Produce and put in an order for a tomato pie. Or two. Possibly three. If I decided I wanted seafood, Chincoteague Shellfish Farms was at the end of the block where I was staying.

One by one I counted off my travel markers: the abandoned ruins of an old roller rink at Chincoteague and Dream Roads, the rocket in front of the NASA Visitor Center, and the enormous gleaming-white satellite dishes that dotted the landscape. Finally I drove onto the narrow, curving road that cut through the channel. Ahead lay Chincoteague, "the beautiful land across the water." The setting sun illuminated the marshes, and I spotted at least a dozen white egrets and some blue herons wading slowly through the shallow water in the early-evening light.

By the time I crossed the bridge, I'd decided to make a quick stop on Main Street and pick up coffee. Maybe I'd buy a bottle of wine for the evening.

The easiest place to park was the lot behind the Village Mall, a big two-story barn-like building with an eclectic assortment of shops on both floors. The entrance is on Main Street, but you can also enter the mall from the parking lot. The shops at the back are devoted to animals in general but cats primarily and feral cats specifically. Some of the side tables along the walkway hold animal cages with soft blankets and towels lining the bottoms. Sometimes there are kittens in the cages and a manager or salesperson will be sitting in a chair and holding one or two kittens, feeding them from baby bottles. One shop has a curtained-off area in the back. At any given time, a litter of kittens might be snuggled together in a basket behind that curtain. The island has an active trap-neuter-return program.

The back of the mall has a bare-metal awning over the double glass doors and two enormous cast-iron lampposts with round, white spheres the size of bowling balls on either side of the doors. As I got out of the car, I noticed a small sign advertising Smith Island BabyCakes propped up against the brick wall.

Mmmm, yum, I thought. I added that to my list as I headed for the door.

The cat was curled up in front of the entrance, the late sun's rays blending in with her orange fur. I was almost on top of her when I heard a raspy meow at my feet and skidded to a halt.

She was small, but not young; I could see now that the fur on her throat and tail was white, sparse, and somewhat spiky. She was skinny, but not starving, ragged, and a little mangy. She rose slowly and limped as she walked. I imagined an incident with a car at some point in her life. Speed limits in Chincoteague top off at twenty-five miles an hour, less in some areas (ducks and geese have the right of way, and I've sat for as long as a quarter of an hour waiting for a gaggle to cross), but animals do get hit and she—the ginger cat—may have been one of them. I pictured her crossing at night, unable to get out of the way. She must have tangled a few times with other cats, too; there were some scratches above her eyes and a tear in her left ear. One eye was cloudy. Blind, probably. The other was perfectly, beautifully, clear and green like the top half of the sea grass that sprouts on the sides of the channel. That eye stared at me.

"Oh, kitty!" I said, and reached down to pet her.

She didn't snarl, just drew back a little and cocked her head to one side. I let my hand drop. She hesitated as though assessing me.

I lifted my hand again, slowly, and offered it to her. She took a step forward and sat. I could almost hear her making the decision: *The hand is kind, not threatening. Safe. She has a nice scent to her.*

She watched me for a few seconds, and then her head dropped back down, as though she had trouble lifting it. I scritched the fur between her ears and she bumped her head against my fingers.

I squatted in front of the ginger and scritched her some more, gently, carefully, under her chin. My knees creaked a little.

The green eye perused me. I caught a glimpse of my own reflection in the glass door. I imagined a thought bubble above the cat's head: *Not young. There are lots of lines on her face.*

"You're one to talk," I replied. The green eye continued to study me.

Red hair pulled back from her face; the top of her head is gray.

"Well, I'm at the beach!" I protested, shifting my weight uncomfortably from knee to knee. "I haven't been able to get to the salon." I caught a glimpse of the BabyCakes sign below my reflection.

I could almost see the thought bubble above the ginger's head: *Could lose a few pounds ...*

"Oh, that's not nice!"

She might be attractive, but she isn't trying as hard as she once did.

"Again," I responded firmly, "I'm at the beach."

The eyes now are still bright. Green eyes. Green like the color of the water in the channel.

Her green eye met mine. There was a pause. She bumped my hand one more time and then rose slowly to her feet. She took a few slow steps.

I stood, also with some difficulty, and glanced around,

wondering if anyone had been watching. The lot was still empty.

"OK, old girl," I said.

She looked up at me briefly.

OK, old girl.

"That's fair," I replied.

I headed into the mall, striding purposefully past the confections displayed on a table by the door and the cacophony of mews coming from one of the stores. When I stepped out onto Main Street, I hesitated and looked back. The hall was dark and the ginger was framed in the back doorway, sitting on her haunches, still watching me. Her front paws were close together, two furry balls of white; from the distance you couldn't see the useless eye and the fading sunlight transformed the pale orangey fur to gold.

I caught a glimpse of my own reflection. The fading light did wonders for me as well.

Still, I would skip dessert.

I dreamed about the ginger that night. She was curled up at the foot of my bed. Suddenly, she rose, arched her back, padded up to me and, staring directly into my face, said (aloud this time): "You're not trying as hard as you once did."

"Well, why should I?" I snapped.

"I wasn't passing judgment," she replied. "Merely stating a fact."

"What's the point?"

"You. *You're* the point."

She took another step closer and began winking at me with her one good eye. It grew brighter and brighter until finally I was jolted from sleep.

Something very bright was flashing in my eyes. It took me a few panicky seconds before I realized what it was: the powerful beam from the Assateague lighthouse, swinging round and round across the water, shining through the sliding glass doors in my bedroom.

One quick look reassured me that the room was animal-free. I got back under the covers. I couldn't get rid of the thought, though. The ginger was right. I wasn't trying as hard as I once did.

The next day I accomplished everything I'd had on my list. By eleven, I was ready to hit the beach. I picked up tacos at Pico Taqueria and stuck them in a small cooler containing fruit and several bottles of water. I set up my umbrella close enough to the water to ensure no one would block my view and read while the crowds arrived and pitched camp around me.

Time passed; I got restless. I polished off one of the tacos (the one with fried oysters and Thai basil) and then did a mile walk on the beach. Upon my return I ate the second taco (this one had crispy cauliflower and shallots) and took the first of three lengthy plunges in the ocean. It was nearly four-thirty when I settled back in my chair and picked up my book again.

Late afternoons are different than mornings at the beach. Quieter. The extended families under canopies have packed up and headed back to get the kids bathed and fed. The remains of sandcastles and holes to China slowly disintegrate. Older couples walk the beach. Younger ones sit on the sand and gaze at the waves and each other. As the crowds thin, singles, like me, become more noticeable. We are of all ages. Most of us are reading books.

I was nearly at the end of mine. I read the last few pages and then packed up, feeling energized.

On the way back to the house, I detoured to Main Street to find something else to read. I knew once I showered and changed I wouldn't feel like going back out. Sandy and damp, I parked behind the mall again. It was a little more crowded than it had been the day before. I looked around for the ginger cat, but she was nowhere to be seen.

I walked the few blocks to Sundial Books and picked out two novels and a biography, perused the local artwork on the walls, and bought a couple of Erick Sahler's postcards (to keep, not send). At the Island Library I picked up flyers and pamphlets about upcoming events. As I left, a fat black cat strolled past me on the porch and sat underneath a chair. I paused at the bronze statue of Misty, the legendary Chincoteague pony, with her companions—a duck and a chicken—and then strolled into the lovely waterfront park behind them.

Families were climbing up on the enormous white Adirondack chairs at the back of the park and arranging themselves beneath the word *LOVE* (a bright-red heart replacing the "V"). I could distinguish at least three separate groups: an older couple with what was probably their daughter and her own two kids, two dads with a toddler, and a mom, dad, and child with a puppy. Cell phones and cameras were happily passed back and forth among relatives and strangers, each happy to play photographer for the others.

The feeling of exclusion was sudden and powerful. It was too late for any of that for me. No partner to grow old with. No children with grandchildren to follow. No big success in life that would afford a place at the beach (the townhouse belonged to a generous friend). The energy I'd felt whooshed out of me like a popped balloon. I left the park and headed back to the mall.

It was dinnertime and the crowds had thinned out. Hardly anyone was in the hallway. I heard loud mewing as I walked past the last store and out into the empty parking lot. I tossed my purchases in the car and opened the door, intending to just go, but then looked back.

There she was, curled up in a ball on the bricks by the side of the door. She lifted her head; it felt as though she'd been waiting for me. I couldn't ignore her.

"Hey there," I said, crouching down.

She cocked her head expectantly, and I obliged with some gentle scritches. She didn't get up this time, but her good eye gleamed at me. She pushed her nose against my fingertip and sniffed.

"I was on the beach," I explained. "Swimming. Walking."

She nudged me. There it was—the thought bubble: *A good smell.*

"Thanks," I said.

Good day?

I was silent.

Another nudge, another look from that vivid green eye.

Good day?

In truth, it had been. Sun. Sand. Ocean. "Sure, fine. I had a good day." I remembered that good friend who'd been happy to offer me her summer place. "A really good day," I added.

Good days are good to have.

"Absolutely. I agree."

One more nudge, then she laid her head back down on her paws and took a deep breath. She let it out and took another. I patted her back. She stretched. We stayed that way for several minutes. When I left she was dozing.

By the end of that first day of the seven days I had in Chincoteague, something had changed. I began doing research for one of the several projects I'd contemplated starting. I went to the beach and made it a point to take a walk and go for a swim. I shopped. I bought more books. I ate out twice and cooked for myself the rest of the time. I spent my mornings on the back porch taking photographs of the egrets and ducks and herons and hummingbirds, and my evenings waiting for the lighthouse to begin its sweep and the glittering stars to appear in the black velvet night.

I didn't dream about the ginger again, but I thought about her. Whenever I went into town, I checked for her in the parking lot. It was usually early morning or late afternoon when I saw her, so I made a point to stop by then. She didn't seem to like crowds; once or twice I thought I caught a glimpse of orange fur disappearing around the back of the building when others were in the parking lot.

I found her supportive of my newfound energy, and our

chats were the most interesting part of my days.

Rest assured, I was fully aware that her thought bubbles were mine. I knew those pep talks weren't emanating from an aging, battered, ginger cat whose life was spent scrabbling to exist, but doesn't that make it even better? I was becoming more positive.

As my departure date moved closer and closer, I did some serious thinking. Over the years I'd had a string of cats, but it had been nearly ten years since the last one died at the age of eighteen. I hadn't considered getting another pet after that. I didn't want to go through that level of grief again. Although I've mourned the loss of family members and friends, all of whom I loved deeply, it's different with pets. They've given themselves over to you with complete devotion. You're in charge; you've become responsible. You hold the power of life and death over them; the final decision is yours. You have to know when it's time. I'd watched the light go out of bright eyes still filled with love for me for the last time.

Or so I thought.

It was two nights before I was due to leave the island. While the sun lowered I sat on the back porch and thought. By the time the lighthouse beam began its spin I knew what I wanted to do.

The ginger cat was going home with me. She didn't have much time left, but I knew that, and I could make her comfortable and pet her and love her and keep her safe for whatever time she did have. Yes, she was in a relatively safe environment. There were bowls of food and water left out at the mall and here on the island, and there were advocates who looked out for wounded cats. But the ginger wasn't wounded; she was just tired and old.

I had no idea whether this was a good idea, but I was going to find out.

I didn't see the ginger when I pulled into the parking lot the next morning. I parked and walked into the mall. There were a few people in the hallway. I glanced in the shop with the curtained-off area in the back. A young woman was standing at the counter, feeding a grayish-black kitten. The kitten was swaddled in a towel, happily sucking on a baby bottle. Both looked up as I entered. The young woman flashed a bright smile.

"Do you need help?" she asked.

"No," I said. "Well, yes. I was interested in one of your cats."

"Sure," she said enthusiastically, nodding toward the back room. I could hear mewing. "We do have kittens now. Most are from a new litter, so they're tiny, but a few are older and have been spayed or neutered. We have a process for adoption. My name's Mary. Give me a couple of minutes to get the paperwork—"

"No, not a kitten. One of the cats outside."

She shook her head, still smiling. "Those aren't *our* cats. We feed them and look out for them but—"

"I understand. I meant … I have a question about the ginger cat."

"Ginger?"

"In the parking lot. She's old and she limps. She's got some white fur mixed in with the orange. One of her ears is torn."

Mary still looked uncertain.

"Her eyes," I said, eagerly. "She's got one bright-green one, the other eye is clouded."

"Oh, of course! Oh, my goodness, yes. We called her GeeGee—kind of a play on 'orange-y'—you know, 'Orange gee.'"

Called. I heard it, but it didn't register. "I was looking for her just now and didn't see her in the lot. I wanted to ask you—"

"She was kind of our mascot," Mary said softly. "She'd been here a long time. We never knew what she'd been through before she came to us. We rarely do."

The mewing from the back room was growing louder. It was distracting, but I was paying sharp attention now.

"She loved sitting in the sun by the door," Mary continued. "Our little streak of sunshine."

I got it.

"You mean …" I drew a shaky breath, wondering whether it had happened during the night or the day before.

She nodded. "It was peaceful. GeeGee just went to sleep and didn't wake up."

"Oh." My heart twisted. I felt tears building. I was too late.

"Everybody asks about her. They still stop by expecting to see her and when they don't—"

"Wait," I said, grasping some but not all of it.

She waited. The swaddled kitten in her arms was dozing.

"When?" I said, finally.

"Oh, about two weeks ago." Mary gently put the kitten back in the cage.

I stared at her.

"Two weeks?" I could barely get the words out.

"At least." She peered at me. "Are you alright?"

I had to get out of there. I mumbled something and stumbled toward the exit, vaguely aware that the mewing behind the curtain had reached a crescendo. Was I losing my mind? What had I been talking to, day after day?

I pushed open the door.

The sun was as bright as it had been my first day. I wondered if the spirit of the ginger cat had remained behind after her weary body had gone to sleep. I wondered if she'd been waiting for something before she let go. I wondered if she'd been waiting for me.

"You come back here!" Mary's voice was sharp.

Was she talking to me?

"The door!"

A sudden flash of orange fur flew toward me. I watched as a small kitten made a mad dash for freedom. I pulled the door shut just in time. The kitten skidded to a halt.

Mary scooped her up and carried her back to the counter; the kitten struggling indignantly. I followed them.

"This one arrived last week," she said, chuffing the yowling kitten under the chin with exasperated affection. "She has a mind of her own. Noisy and feisty and not terribly friendly."

The kitten glared at her and then looked at me with bright-green eyes. She grew silent and still. I noticed the fur on her throat was white and her front paws were white.

"Well, how about that?" Mary slowly released the kitten on the counter and stepped back. The kitten and I perused each other, and I noticed a tiny nip in one of her ears.

The ginger kitten's eyes met mine. She took one cautious step toward me and stopped. She waited.

Several nights ago, in a dream, I'd asked: "What's the point?" The response, from the spirit of a tired, battered ginger cat was: "You. *You're* the point."

Maybe it wasn't just me.

I cleared my throat. "You mentioned there was a process."

Mary nodded.

"Let's start it."

The tiny ginger stepped closer and bumped her head against my hand.

"Now."

Linda Chambers teaches scriptwriting at Carver Center for the Arts and writes for both theater and film. She collaborates with the Young Filmmakers Workshop as an acting coach and screenwriter and is also working on an adaptation of *The Emperor's New Clothes* for Pumpkin Children's Theatre. The continuing saga of *The Swords of Ialmorgia*, her fantasy novel, is available on Amazon Kindle, with more adventures on the way. "The Ginger" is Linda's third short story to be published by Cat & Mouse Press (see *Beach Pulp* and *Beach Life*). She dedicates this to Bubbles, "the last one", who crossed the rainbow bridge at age eighteen, many years ago.

My Daughter Teaches Every Child She Knows to Love Her Cat

by Alice Morris

He was a half-grown stray, regularly ripped to shreds
by the mangy pack of oversized ferals that had the run

of the old,
beat-down, seaside Lewes neighborhood.

Early each morning he'd show up outside our cottage door–
crying, shaking, bleeding.

My three-year-old watched as I left him a little milk,
a bit of bread, a nip of cheese.

I'd tell my daughter *stay back*, explain
disease.

Eventually, she had to touch the copper-colored fur
on his back,

and as though he knew he had found his home, his girl,
he never left a scratch.

We named him Penny because of his color, and because
it seemed his cat world believed

he had no value.
But my child endlessly played with, talked about,

and drew pictures of our newfound Penny.
Soon, he appeared in other children's family drawings.

I first wrote this poem for a Lost and Found Poetry and Prose Series, initially thinking I would write about a diamond lost from a ring, but then I was flooded with memories and images of Penny, who first came to us, really, as a refugee cat in desperate need of sanctuary. I am so glad Penny is able to have another cat-life in this collection dedicated to cats and dogs. May Penny soon appear in your family drawings.

Alice Morris, MS in counseling from Johns Hopkins, is a Pushcart Prize and Best of the Net nominee. She comes to writing with a background in art and has been published in *The New York Art Review* and *West Virginia Studies Our Heritage*. In 2018, she won the Florence C. Coltman Award for Creative Writing and was shortlisted in a *Postcard Poetry and Prose* contest. She attended the 2018 Seaside Writers Retreat. In 2019, she won second place (single poem) and third place (single short story) in the Delaware Press Association Communications Contest. Her poem, "Watercress," was a finalist for the 2019 Art of Stewardship Pat Herold Nielsen Poetry Prize. Recently, her work was noted by Goodreads reviewer Jeffrey Keeten. Her writing appears or is forthcoming in numerous anthologies and in *The Broadkill Review, Paterson Literary Review, Backbone Mountain Review, Rat's Ass Review, Gargoyle,* and other publications.

It Happened One Night

by D.M. Domosea

To this day, no one knows exactly how it happened, only that it did, and that the inhabitants of 1235 Maryland Avenue would never be the same. At least the non-human inhabitants, to include a finicky long-haired calico by the name of Clawdette Colbert and a rambunctious boxer named Barkley Gable. The man and woman, their respective human owners, met a year prior and bonded over a shared love of old Hollywood movies and bad puns. Neither pet cared much for the other, yet in the months after their Cape May households were combined, Clawdette and Barkley achieved a fragile détente based on mutual avoidance.

The evening before the event, now referred to only as The Bad Time, started out much the same as every other. Clawdette curled into the woman's lap for a post-dinner stroking session on the couch, while Barkley rested at the man's feet, as he watched television in a room designated as the man cave. That particular evening, the man took to shouting at the screen—something about a bad call on the play—which

Barkley found ill-suited for his post-dinner nap. He left the man cave and took up a spot on the couch next to the woman.

That was mistake number one.

Clawdette found the intrusion intolerable, especially since the woman now divided her strokes between the two. Plus, Barkley stank, which soured the otherwise relaxing atmosphere. Affronted by both the odor and the blatant disregard for her sacred bonding time with the woman, Clawdette jumped from the woman's lap. She strutted across the room to the one space in the house that belonged to Barkley alone: an overstuffed black-and-red dog bed. With a furtive glance at the couch to ensure she had the proper audience, Clawdette hopped in.

Barkley curled his upper lip. He couldn't believe Clawdette had committed such a blatant act of aggression. After all, it's not like he'd pushed her off the woman's lap. He'd lain in a spot that otherwise sat empty, only somewhat near to Clawdette's spot. It certainly didn't warrant this level of sacrilege. However, Barkley was willing to let it go, as he was now able to place his head in the space vacated by the cat.

That single act ignited a pettiness within Clawdette that went well beyond that typical of most calicos. She needed to deal with this offense promptly if she was to retain the upper hand in their household. Clawdette wormed her way under the bed's cushion until only her bushy tail stuck out, then emerged on the other side, dragging with her a bone. Barkley's one-hundred-percent-genuine rawhide beef bone.

That was mistake number two.

Barkley leapt from the couch, bounded over the coffee

table, and landed at the foot of his bed. Clawdette darted from the cushion. She sprang up the back of the recliner and over to the top of the bookcase. Barkley scrabbled across the hardwood floor after her.

You touched my bone!

Oh, did I? My sincere apologies. I only meant to determine what unsightly piece of garbage might be stuck under your bed.

You know full well that's where I keep my bone, and you're not allowed to touch it.

And you know full well the woman's lap is mine after the evening meal. You drove me away with your incessant mouth-breathing and foul stench.

I don't have a stench. You do. Like old litter box and bad fish. You are a spoiled-rotten diva.

And you are a waste of space and oxygen.

Of course, the entire exchange—as viewed by the humans—consisted only of thunderous barks and growling hisses.

"Hey now, boy. Calm down." The man, who'd dashed into the living room to check on the cause of the ruckus, kneeled at Barkley's side and rubbed his ears. "What set him off?"

The woman shrugged. "Clawdette messed with his bone. You know how protective of it he is."

"Well, she's not touching it now, see Barkley?" The man pulled the bone from the bed and offered it to the agitated boxer. Barkley whined once before grabbing it and retreating into his bed. "There, all better, right?"

The man reached to scratch the cat's ears, but Clawdette

was now in no mood for contact and moved her head away.

As the humans retired to their bedroom for the night, they heard a final growl, answered by a feline hiss.

You are a lazy, pampered pest, good for nothing but sleeping and pooping.

And you are a vile interloper and brownnosing brute.

With that parting shot, Clawdette made herself cozy atop the bookcase, purring herself into a trance that eventually deepened into sleep, while Barkley drifted off, paws wrapped around his rawhide bone.

Sometime later, Clawdette woke for a pre-dawn prowl of the kitchen. She noticed that what should have been the solid wood of the bookcase was softer than it should be. It also reeked of dog. She opened her eyes and found herself not only at floor level, but also in the middle of the dog's bed, wrapped around the rawhide bone. She panicked and tried to leap from the bed but found her body less lithe than usual and so tumbled out instead.

Clawdette glanced around for the dog, and—satisfied he was nowhere near—set to washing off whatever post-sleep funk weighed her down. She lifted a dainty white paw and was met instead with a large, rough-padded, black foot. She switched to the other forepaw, only to find it the same. A white bib of short, coarse hair had replaced her fluffy tuft of silken chest fur, and her tail—her beautiful tail—was now a brown stub.

What's happening?

As Clawdette struggled to make sense of the situation,

Barkley, who'd been dreaming of chasing a ball in the ocean waves, woke with a start when the dream wave crashed over his head. He pushed himself to standing and immediately noticed his bed was missing. Even more alarming was the fact that the floor next to his bed also was gone, a fact he registered only as he fell a considerable distance before hitting it.

Barkley landed on his feet and stared up at the cat's perch from where he'd fallen. Somehow, that calculating feline must have dragged him up there while he slept, which made no sense but seemed in keeping with the cat's nature, if not her capability. However, that accounted for neither the strange, claustrophobic feeling that now plagued him nor the suffocating pouf of fur in his face.

What's happening?

Startled by the question, Barkley and Clawdette turned and found themselves face to face with … themselves. Or something that looked just like themselves.

Clawdette snarled at the doppelganger standing before her and was stunned to discover her melodious soprano replaced with a crude and piteous dog-like howl:

Get out, you feral peasant. This is my home, and you are not welcome here.

Barkley raised his hackles in response. He barked a warning at the strange dog that looked just like him, but the warning came out as an embarrassingly high-pitched mewl:

Your home? This is my home, trespasser. Now leave before I bite you.

Bite me and I'll claw your eyes out, you vile interloper.

Vile interloper? The voice was off and the body was different, but something in the haughty words rang familiar to Barkley. Could it be? He inched closer to the other boxer and tilted his head.

Wait … pampered pest? Is that you?

Clawdette gasped. Only one creature dared to call her that.

Brownnosing brute? Why do you look like me?

Why do you look like me?

In that moment, the animals realized their bodies had been inexplicably switched.

Barkley accused the cat of evil spells, while Clawdette blamed the mess on the dog's tendency for clumsy collisions. Outrageous charges and bitter insults hurtled between the two. The commotion woke the humans and brought them rushing into the living room, where they found the calico and boxer in a vicious standoff.

"What's going on? Barkley, leave the kitty alone!" The woman grabbed for Barkley's collar, but the boxer whined and fled for the safety of the sunroom. The calico scampered over to the man and wagged its tail at his feet.

"Guess he's still sore about the rawhide." The man scratched the calico's head. "Best give him his space, OK, Clawdette?"

The humans moved to the kitchen to start the day with a pot of coffee, leaving behind—unbeknownst to them—an agitated dog stuffed inside the body of the cat and an anxious cat imprisoned in the body of the dog.

Confusion and hostility dampened the mood of the entire

household in the week following. The sudden bizarre change in their pets' behaviors increased tensions between the humans. The woman couldn't understand why the normally social and eager-to-please boxer stayed scarce for most of the day, hiding in nooks and crannies into which he barely fit, while the calico's tendency to now be underfoot, along with her non-stop attempts to escape outside, irritated the man. They both found the constant snarling and hissing between the two animals worrisome.

Things came to a decisive head on the sixth day of The Bad Time. When coaxed to sit in exchange for a doggy snack, Clawdette yawned, arched her back to the extent she could in the dog's body, and sauntered out of the kitchen. She had never cared for the pungent smell or taste of the dog's snacks and certainly wouldn't perform a trick for one. Barkley, on the other hand, sat, offered a shake, rolled over, and played dead in hopes of earning a treat or two, all of which were disregarded by the man.

"Fine. If you're not going to listen, then you don't need these," the man said to the boxer's retreating tail. He stowed the bag on the highest shelf of the pantry and left the kitchen.

That was the last straw for Barkley.

In the space of a week, Clawdette had ruined everything for him. Morning beach walks with the man? Gone. Special treats for well-executed tricks? Ignored. Evening strolls along the boardwalk? Canceled. Barkley's leash now hung on the hook by the door, unused.

Clawdette refused to go any farther than the backyard to relieve herself, and that was only under protest, as the humans, naturally assuming she was the boxer, prevented her from using the litter box.

It never occurred to the man to leash the calico for a sandy stroll along the Cape May shore, even if that cat wanted nothing more in the world than to frolic in the waves. Clawdette had expressly forbidden Barkley that option anyway, as the saltwater might ruin her coat.

The sound of running water coming from down the hallway gave Barkley an idea. He trotted toward the bathroom and nudged his way through the door. The woman stood before the mirror, tying up her hair. Barkley crept in and leapt onto the tub's rim. Above all things, Clawdette prized her luxurious coat. It was her pride and joy, her height of vanity. When this body belonged to her, she spent hours each day cleaning it. She'd be livid if anything were to happen to it while under his control. So, Barkley jumped in. The drenched coat alone was beyond the pale, but this was only part one of Barkley's plan.

The commotion startled the woman, who turned and cried out, "Clawdette! What are you doing, you crazy cat?"

Barkley scrambled out of the tub, resisted the urge to shake off the excess water, and zoomed out of the bathroom and down the hall. On his way, he passed Clawdette, who'd just woken up to investigate.

What are you—?

Barkley didn't stop.

Clawdette followed the trail of water to the laundry room. There, she found the dog standing in front of her litter box, dripping water from her coat (*her* coat!) onto the tile floor.

Barkley turned as Clawdette unleashed her rage.

What have you done? My coat! My beautiful, clean coat!

Barkley took a step back and placed his hind paws into the litter box.

Whoa. Wait now. What are you doing?

I've had it, cat. You've ruined play time, snack time, nap time; you've ruined everything I love; so now that I'm in your body, I'm going to ruin everything you love.

OK, wait. Stop. I know we don't see eye to eye, but you can't seriously mean to ...

Barkley inched backward and placed his front paws on the top edge of the box.

Wait, please! You've gotten my fur soaked and ...

Barkley dropped his front paws in.

It's clumping litter!

And with that, Barkley dropped and wallowed inside the box, covering his feline coat from tail to ears with pebbly bits of clay that melted and stuck to the fur.

Clawdette collapsed onto the tile as she bemoaned the ruination of her beautiful, silky coat, destroyed by the charlatan that now inhabited her body. She wanted to flounder in despair. To wallow in misery over the loss of everything she loved about being a cat. Her sleek feline agility. Her regal floof of chest fur. Her ability to scale the curtains.

Yes, she wanted to despair, but she was a cat. No matter that she was cursed with this foul meat sack of a dog body. She was still a cat to her core, and cats didn't wallow and flounder. Cats schemed. Cats retaliated. Cats got even. And she knew exactly how to do it.

Clawdette pulled herself together and marched into the living room, straight to the dog's bed. The pressure inside her lower belly told her a potty break could easily be induced. With the man out on errands and the woman submerged in her bath and music, she had the perfect, plausible excuse for what happened next. Clawdette climbed into the black-and-red dog bed and squatted.

The front door opened and closed, followed by the sound of footsteps heading her way. Clawdette stepped out of the bed and waited defiantly next to it.

"Hey, boy. Are you ready to—" The man rounded the corner and stopped. He looked from the bed to the boxer and back to the bed. "What the hell happened here?"

A substantial brown turd—one Clawdette could never produce with her compact feline body—sat squarely in the middle of the cushion, surrounded by a wet, pungent circle that spread over half the circumference of the bed.

"What is it? What's wrong?" The woman appeared next to him, wrapped in a bathrobe.

"Just look at what he's done!" The man pointed at the bed.

The woman frowned. "Accidents happen, hon. Did you not walk him this morning?"

"No, he didn't want to go. He never wants to go anymore."

The woman huffed and turned toward the kitchen. "So, I'll clean it up, and then we'll wash—Oh, my God!"

Clawdette, who'd been sizing up the intractable mess she'd made of the dog's bed with no small modicum of pride, looked in the direction of the scream and followed suit with a howl of her own.

Barkley pranced into the room in the calico's body, but gone were the soft patches of black, gray, and orange. The cat's coat was now covered with a shell of dull clay. A leaden masque weighed down the once jaunty tail, and was that ... Yes, a nugget of day-old poop topped the end like a pennant of shame.

But Barkley's smug walk lasted only until the smell hit his nose. The gagging odor of the somewhat used litter caked all over his body overwhelmed him, but the signature scent of his own calling card was unmistakable. He glared at the cat as he tiptoed past her and peered into his bed.

You … you pooped in my bed?

Technically, since this is your body, you did it.

And my bone? You peed on my bone?

Did I? Oh, tsk, tsk. I forgot it was there.

Barkley slashed out with the calico's needle-sharp claws and swiped the nose that had once been his. Three red welts bloomed across the black muzzle. Clawdette snarled in turn, bearing the boxer's yellowed, saliva-slicked teeth back at him.

How dare you desecrate my sleeping place with your filthy habits.

How dare I? How dare you! You started this when you jumped into that bath, you mouth-panting cretin.

No, you started it the moment you moved in here, you pretentious, butt-licking snob!

You think I wanted to move in with you? Things were going just fine for me and—

A door slammed. Only then did the animals realize the humans had left the room. With their growling and hissing at each other now on pause, the sound of another confrontation echoed down the hallway. Curious, Clawdette and Barkley went to listen at the bedroom door.

"I don't know what to do, either. They're obviously not getting along," said the woman.

"We can't keep on like this. They're going to hurt each other, or worse. We can't keep them in the same house."

"So, what are you saying? We should give one of them away?"

Barkley and Clawdette glanced at each other.

"No, I … no. Not give away, but maybe forcing them into this was a mistake."

The woman's voice, soft and fragile, asked "What are you saying?"

"I don't know. Maybe … maybe this just isn't working out for us." A long period of silence followed.

No. Not this. Clawdette had heard these kinds of words before and knew it meant confusion and disruption and horribly sad humans. Clawdette cut an accusatory look at the dog that wore her body and then crept back down the hallway, leaving Barkley alone to listen to the sound of his owner crying on the other side of the door.

Sometime later, after the man thoroughly scrubbed the clay from the calico's fur and then disappeared into the man cave with an armful of pillows and sheets, a damp Barkley searched out the feline. He found her crammed into the space under the wicker armchair in the sunroom.

What's wrong with the humans?

Barkley worried Clawdette might not answer him. She stared blankly at the opposite wall, not bothering to acknowledge him, but after a few stark moments, she spoke.

The man had another mate before he met your owner. They were happy, too, at first, but they started to growl at each other more and more every day. Then the woman left, and everything changed. She packed her clothes inside a canvas bag and never came back. I loved that bag—it was one of my favorite places to curl up.

But you and the man were OK, right?

Yes, but he was sad for a long time. I gave him more attention, but I could tell he was still lonely. That changed when he met your owner.

The woman was also lonely until your owner came along.

Clawdette blinked at him but said nothing. They lay together in silence, absorbed in their thoughts, until Barkley stirred and sat upright.

I want our humans to be happy, and I think they can be again if we find a way to live with each other.

It's more than just living with each other now. It's living as each other. How do we do that?

Maybe if I show you how to be a good dog, you can teach me how to be a better cat.

Deep into the night, as their owners slept in separate rooms, Clawdette and Barkley shared all there was to know about being the best of each other. Clawdette balked at the idea of jumping to catch an ocean-soaked toy midair, while Barkley dreaded the boredom of endless napping. But with the threat of their owners' sorrow looming over them, the pets of 1235 Maryland Avenue, Cape May, New Jersey, proved to be willing learners.

The next morning, Barkley resisted the urge to whine at the front door and dash out anytime it was opened, as he had taken to doing the past week. Instead, he found the brightest sunbeam on the sunroom floor and curled up in it.

And when the woman opened the back door to let the boxer out for his morning potty break, Clawdette declined. She trotted over to the dog's leash hanging by the front door and pawed at it, just as Barkley instructed. The humans—who had yet to speak to each other that morning—exchanged surprised looks.

"I'll take him," the man offered.

"No, I'll go."

In the end, they both went. Clawdette could never say she truly enjoyed that morning at the beach. The open space and chaos of activity nearly stressed her to her limit, and her jumps to catch the toy were half-hearted at best, but the way the woman's laughter elicited a smile from the man pleased Clawdette greatly.

That first day of The Great Truce was not a perfect peace, but rather a perfect attempt at one, and the tensions eased between the humans as the animals returned to semi-normal behavior. Over the course of that time, Clawdette and Barkley each grew to appreciate what it meant to be a dog and a cat to the humans who loved them.

On the fifth night of The Great Truce, as the humans retired to their room, Barkley slipped over to his old bed, which had been washed five times to rid it of the unfortunate smell. The rawhide bone had been unsalvageable. Clawdette lay curled up in the middle of the cushion.

Don't take this the wrong way, but I think that being a cat maybe isn't as bad as I thought.

Oh? In what way?

This body is just the right size to fit in the woman's lap, so that's nice. The chin scratching is good, too, and I can tell it soothes her. She enjoys it, and that makes me happy.

Anything else?

I'll never get used to all the fluff on this body, but the way it soaks up a sunbeam's warmth makes for a good snooze.

Clawdette acknowledged his compliment with a sniff and closed her eye again. As the dog turned to leave, she stopped him with her own observation.

The man really enjoys those morning walks with me—I mean, you—on the beach. I hadn't realized how much until this past week.

Walks are fun. Especially the chasing and jumping parts.

I wouldn't call it fun, but the man's reaction to it is satisfying. Besides, the sand is basically one big litter box, and I like the fishy smell of the water. I think I can manage it.

They left it at that. Clawdette resettled herself into the dog bed, while Barkley took up one of the cat's many preferred sleeping nooks on the back of the couch. From across the room, as Clawdette snuggled into the padding, the dog called to her once more.

Clawdette?

Yes, Barkley?

I think this could be the beginning of a beautiful friendship.

As the moon made its own lazy jump over the sleeping town of Cape May, the bridge now forged between the former foes allowed for another crossing, with each unconsciously returning to their proper place.

D.M. Domosea has an unquenchable thirst for geekable speculative fiction in all forms. Her work can be found online and in various anthologies, including *Beach Pulp* and *Beach Dreams* from Cat & Mouse Press. She is currently in the query trenches with a middle grade novel and eyeing up the next project from her overflowing story nursery. D.M. lives in the dwindling woodlands of Maryland with her family, who has yet to realize a solar-powered clone replaced her three years ago. You can find more of her work online at www.dmdomosea.com.

Midnight's Treasures

by Doretta Warnock

*V*alerie, did you bring the mail in today?" asked Hank.

"No, dear. I forgot. I'll get it now." Valerie was forgetting a lot of things these days. Her head hadn't been screwed on right since Chantilly died.

Valerie strolled into the foyer, pausing to look at the picture of Chantilly. Her white Pekingese, with a red ball clenched tightly in her small mouth, stared back at her. Valerie remembered how easy it was to pick a name for the dog. Her long, curly, white hair looked just like Chantilly lace. She also recalled why she forgot the mail today. Chantilly always let her know when the mail arrived. That dog hated people dressed in uniforms. She would yap incessantly to announce the arrival of the mail.

Valerie opened the heavy front door and scooped the mail from the box on the front porch. The wind slammed the lid shut. She hurried inside, kicking the door closed with her foot before the wind could blow grass clippings into the house. She raked through the mail. No bills today. That was good, but too many catalogs. She wondered how many trees were killed making these advertisements that she would never read. She dropped them into the recycle bin, and a greeting card fell to the parquet floor. How did she miss it? She glanced at the return label. It was from Debbie, her widowed neighbor across the street.

She opened the pink envelope, revealing a sympathy card inside. A sympathy card for the loss of her dog; that was a first. She thought about the dogs she had lost in her lifetime. Never had anyone sent her a card. Debbie was so thoughtful. Valerie slipped on her flip-flops and strolled across the street to thank Debbie for her kindness.

"Come around back; I'm on the porch," Debbie yelled, in answer to the doorbell.

Valerie walked around the house. Debbie, already clad in her pajamas and robe, sat in her Adirondack chair with a glass of red wine in her hand. "Care to join me for a glass of wine? You're just in time to see our beautiful Bethany Beach sunset."

"Sure." Valerie didn't want to make this a long visit, but she could use a friend. And the sunsets were indeed better on Debbie's side of the street. Valerie had barely sat when Debbie returned with another glass of wine.

"I just wanted to thank you for the sympathy card. That was so thoughtful."

"You're welcome. People without pets don't understand how people grieve when their pets die. They're part of the family," Debbie said.

"I didn't know you have a dog."

"I don't. I have a cat."

Valerie frowned.

"I can tell by the look on your face you're not a cat lover."

"You're right—I'm not. Cats don't show affection, and they don't come when you call them. I'll take a dog anytime."

"I beg to differ. Midnight! Midnight, come here."

A cat squeezed under the lattice framework from beneath the porch. He was completely black except for a small patch of white fur resembling a crescent moon on his left front paw. Valerie smiled. It was the perfect name for him. Cat lovers know how to pick great names too. She thought about Chantilly again.

"Oh, what's that?" Valerie watched Midnight drop what appeared to be a dead bird at Debbie's feet.

"That's how cats thank you for taking care of them. They leave you presents." Debbie picked up Midnight and plopped him on Valerie's lap. "Here, hold him while I clean this up. Don't be afraid. Just stroke him like this. He might not wag his tail like a dog, but soon he will show you affection."

Valerie followed Debbie's lead. Sure enough, Midnight curled up in Valerie's lap, purring like a steam engine.

"See, he likes you. Hey, I have a great idea. I'm going to Florida for a week to visit my brother and I'm in a pinch. How would you like to take care of Midnight for me? He's not much trouble. He's mostly an outdoor cat. You only have to keep his bowls full of water and cat food."

Valerie hesitated. "Well—"

"If you have any trouble, the Cummingses can help you. They have two cats; they'll know what to do."

"Aren't they in Hawaii?"

"Yes, but they'll be back in three days. I leave tomorrow morning. You'll only be on your own for two days."

Valerie wasn't sure how her husband, Hank, would feel about this, but she paused only a moment before agreeing.

"Great. I'll leave cat food in my garage and the bowl outside the door so Midnight can get it anytime he wants. Just bring him into your house at night and let him out in the morning."

The next day, Valerie walked across the street to fill Midnight's bowl. She opened the bag of cat food and poured two scoops into the bowl. Was that enough? Debbie hadn't told her how many scoops he would eat. She thought she read somewhere that cats were smart enough not to overeat, and she didn't want to underfeed him. She dumped one more scoop into the bowl, filling it to the brim. She saw Midnight come around the corner of the garage and freeze. She figured he was waiting for her to leave. Satisfied that he would eat, Valerie walked home.

In the evening, Valerie returned to get Midnight. The bowl was empty, but there was no sign of him. She called his name several times, but he wouldn't come. So much for cats coming when you call them. She peered under the porch, but it was dark. After calling his name three more times, she gave up. Midnight would have to spend the night outside. It was a good thing it was a warm summer evening.

Valerie had a restless night. Who would have thought she would be worried about a stupid cat? At the first sign of light, she put on her pink bathrobe and tied the belt snuggly around her waist. She opened the front door only to be greeted by a dead rat lying on the porch. She screamed and Hank came running.

"Are you alright?"

Valerie pointed at the rat.

"Now what kind of prank is that? Darn kids."

"I don't think it was kids. I think Debbie's cat brought me a present."

"Well, it was your idea to watch the cat, so you can bury it. I'm going back to bed," Hank said, as he rubbed his eyes.

Valerie buried the rat and ran to Debbie's house to find Midnight. "Midnight, where are you? Come here." When he didn't appear, she rattled the cat food bag and called louder.

A man in the rental property next door opened a window and yelled, "Hey, lady, it's six in the morning. Keep your voice down. Some of us are still sleeping."

"I'm sorry." He was right. She refilled the bowls and walked home listlessly. Should she call Debbie and tell her the cat was missing? Valerie decided to wait until tonight to see if Midnight would reappear.

He didn't, but the bowl was empty again. That was a good sign. She convinced herself there was no need to call Debbie. She would try to get a good night's sleep and reassess the situation in the morning.

Valerie slept a little later the next day. She made a cup of tea in her favorite mug, the one with a picture of Chantilly. It took a few sips before she felt ready to face her problem. She opened the front door slowly. There was no dead rat, but today there was a coconut on the porch. Valerie laughed. Not a little laugh, but a deep, bellowing laugh, the kind that relieved all her stress. Midnight was alive and well and playing games with her. Chantilly never did anything like this. Was Debbie right? Are cats more fun than dogs? Was Valerie turning into a cat person?

Now she had a new problem. Who did the coconut belong to? She glanced at the Cummingses' house. Their blue Lexus was back in the driveway, so they must be back from their trip. Valerie rang their doorbell. Bill Cummings, whose skin was so tan it looked like leather, answered the door. She held up the coconut. "Bill, does this belong to you?"

"Probably. I dropped a bag of coconuts when I unpacked the car and some of them rolled under the car. I thought I picked them all up, but I guess I missed one. Where did you get it?"

"Debbie's cat delivered it to my door."

The neighbor chuckled. "How did you know it was mine?"

"It wasn't hard to solve. You're the only people on the street who went to Hawaii."

"Well, thank you very much. I make an awesome coconut rum punch. The next time I make it, I'll have you and Hank over to share it."

"Sounds good. And I want to see your pictures."

"You got it."

Valerie was more relaxed. Her blood pressure was probably down ten points. She had felt good enough to spend the day on Bethany Beach with Hank. They jumped the waves, walked the boardwalk, and had ice cream. She didn't think about Midnight at all. In fact, when they got home, she almost forgot to look for him. He still wouldn't come when she called, so she refilled his bowl. He was going to spend another night outside.

The next morning, Valerie couldn't wait to see if Midnight had left her another treasure. She opened the front door and found a set of keys. Dangling from a key chain were a tiny kaleidoscope, a house key, and a key and remote with Chevrolet logos. Valerie closed one eye and peered into the kaleidoscope. She saw a happy family of four standing in front of the Eiffel Tower. There was so much sand embedded in the grooves it was hard to see the faces. All she could tell was that the father was tall and had a healthy head of curly hair. He reminded her of Art Garfunkel. Clearly, somebody had lost these keys on the beach.

Valerie got dressed quickly and ran down the street haphazardly, zapping the remote at every Chevy she could find. She roamed four blocks before she realized that this was futile. There were way too many Chevys, and this would only help her find the car, not its owner. Plus, what if she was able to unlock a car? If the owner were nearby, he might think she was stealing it.

She took a shortcut home, cutting through her neighbors' yards, jumped into her Ford truck, and drove to the Bethany Beach police station. Inside, she saw a man, a woman, and two children huddled around the sergeant's desk. She couldn't miss the father's wild hair. She heard him say, "Did anyone turn them in?"

"Is this what you're looking for?" Valerie said, as she held up the keys.

The man turned and grinned. He hugged Valerie so hard she dropped the keys.

"Where did you find them?"

"I didn't. A cat did. They're covered in sand. You must have dropped them on the beach."

"They must have fallen out of my beach bag."

"Well, mystery solved," said the sergeant. His uniform was so tight Valerie was surprised he could speak.

Her attention turned to the Art Garfunkel look-alike. "Have a safe trip home."

"Will do, and thanks again."

In bed that night, Valerie felt cocky. Her mind raced. Today was the second time someone had thanked her for solving a mystery. Maybe she should start a detective agency. Midnight could be her sidekick and bring her cases to solve. But he wasn't her cat. Debbie would be home tomorrow. Maybe she would go to the animal shelter and adopt her own cat. Cats *were* more fun than dogs.

Valerie woke the next morning and opened her front door, hoping to find one last treasure from Midnight. There, on the porch, was a yellow bikini bottom. That was one mystery she didn't want to solve. She looked at her picture of Chantilly Lace again. Today, she was going to the animal shelter to adopt a dog.

Doretta Warnock was born and raised in New Jersey. She recently relocated to southern Delaware with her husband to be near the beach. Although she has no pets, this story was inspired by a collection of true stories involving the pets of family and friends. This is her third publication. She also wrote "How to Give an Alligator a Bath," which was published in *Fun for Kidz* magazine and "Oil and Vinegar," which appeared in *Calliope*, Mensa's literary magazine.

Saving Matilda

by Susan Miller

She always wanted to be
the tough girl, the one who
walked barefoot across
the boardwalk at the beach.
The one whose eyes winked
under sky-blue shadow, whose
mouth pouted with rose gloss.
The one who madly whizzed
around in Funland's bumper cars
in a meager, star-spangled
bikini, the one who giggled
on the Gravitron or carelessly
whipped bleach-baby locks
into the air while others
screamed on the Superflip.
The one who sneaked
cigarettes with sulking boys
before precisely shooting
a Skee-ball with a delicate,
rope-bracelet-wrapped wrist.
The one whose triple mint
chip from Archie's never dripped,
the one whose golden fingers
never got greased beneath
a bucket of Thrasher's fries.
But she was this girl.

The one whose walker
wheels caught crags
in wooden planks, whose
thick rubber shoes plodded
along each morning to her
perch on a bench outside
Dolle's. The one whose aging
Persian purred and curled
on the lap of her polyester
master, always there,
saving Matilda, gently easing
fleeting dreams that still swirled
on searing summer days
like all those others,
the lost decades before.

She would never be
the tough girl, the one who
walked barefoot across
the boardwalk at the beach.

Susan Miller is an editor/reporter for *USA TODAY* newspaper who enjoys creative writing as a hobby. Her poetry has appeared in several publications, including *Common Ground Review, Gemini Magazine, Months and Years,* and *Under the Bridges of America.* She is an annual visitor to the Delaware beaches and had a short story published in *Beach Life* (Cat & Mouse Press) in 2017.

Finding Sunshine

by Robin Hill-Page Glanden

*Y*ou should get away," Connie said. "Get out of that house and away from everything that reminds you of Marc or medical stuff. Get a change of scenery and a fresh perspective on your life. Some time at my beach condo would do you a world of good."

On her fortieth birthday, Christina found the car—and the man—of her dreams in a Mazda showroom. Marc Carson was the breathtakingly handsome salesman who sold Christina a sporty new car and stole her heart.

There was a whirlwind romance and a beautiful wedding. It all seemed like a dream come true to Christina. But just three months into their marriage, Marc quit his job, saying he was unhappy working in sales. After months of unemployment, he got a job as a bartender in a popular Wilmington restaurant. Their life together seemed perfect. Until her annual mammogram.

The radiologist detected "an area of concern." Three weeks later, Christina underwent surgery, and her whole world turned upside down. Although the surgery went well, her follow-up treatment included chemotherapy, and that was rough. Christina got sick and lost her hair. As the weeks of treatment wore on, she felt Marc pulling away from her. When she tried to talk about her illness, he changed the subject.

One night, Marc came home and told her he was leaving. He said he hadn't signed up for life as the caretaker for a sick wife. Christina discovered later he was having an affair with a hostess at the restaurant. He filed for divorce and went to live with his new (and younger) girlfriend.

Family and friends stepped up to help with rides, meals, and errands. But even after chemo ended, Christina felt like she was sleepwalking through each day. She struggled to pull her shattered life together. She was now a middle-aged woman with ugly scars, a bald head, and no husband.

Christina's first week in Rehoboth consisted mostly of watching old movies and sleeping. But her sleep was anything but peaceful. Disturbing images haunted her dreams—people in black robes sticking needles in her arms, Marc yelling at her, and her townhouse burning.

Each morning, Christina sat on the balcony of the condo to get sun and fresh air and to enjoy the ocean view, but the people she saw on the boardwalk depressed her. Couples walking by holding hands reminded her of the love she had lost. She was so damaged now that no man would ever want her. Kids ran by, laughing. She would never have kids. Families were everywhere, enjoying time together on summer vacation. She would never have a family of her own. Everyone looked so happy and healthy. Would she ever look and feel good again?

Even though her oncologist said her prognosis was excellent, the worry was a constant, nagging ache.

In the second week, Christina left the condo. Her craving for a good cup of coffee and a bagel forced her out of hiding. She dressed in faded denim jeans and pulled on a large, loose, cotton tunic. A wide-brimmed straw fedora covered her short, white, spikey hair. She walked up Rehoboth Avenue to Starbucks. The steaming cup of Pike Place was nirvana.

Back at the condo, as she fumbled with the door key, she felt something brush against her leg. She heard a faint squeaking sound. She looked down and saw a tiny, yellow, tiger-striped kitten at her feet. The kitten looked up at her and squeaked again.

"Well, what are *you* doing out *here*?" Christina said. "It's not safe for a baby like you to be wandering around outside. Go back home." The kitten didn't budge. Christina opened the door to the condo and the kitten darted inside.

"No! Stop!"

The kitten made a beeline for the kitchen, and Christina followed as it ran with a strange, hopping gait and scooted under the kitchen table.

"Come on, kitty," she pleaded. The kitten stared at her with large, green eyes. "You came to the wrong house," Christina said. "I'm not a cat person."

The tiny kitten cowered under the table beyond Christina's reach, but she figured she could lure it out with tuna. As soon as she popped the can lid and the kitten caught a whiff, it ran out and started to devour the food. It was then that Christina noticed the kitten was missing its right front paw.

"Hey, little kitty, what happened to you?" Christina sat down on the floor next to the kitten and called Connie.

"Hi," Connie said. "Is everything OK?"

"Yes, I'm fine, but I have a situation here," said Christina.

"What's up?"

"Do any of your neighbors have cats?"

"Not that I know of. Why?"

"Well, a kitten was at the door today and ran inside. I gave it tuna and it's eating like there's no tomorrow. It's missing a front paw. It seems OK, but I don't know what to do."

"There's a magnet on the fridge with Doc Carney's number and address. He's the vet for our cat, Chico. Dr. Carney and his wife have an office right there in Rehoboth. Does the kitten have a collar?"

"No."

"It might have a chip. The vet can check and maybe locate the owner. If not, you might have a new little friend." Connie chuckled.

"Oh, noooo. I can barely take care of myself these days. I don't need an animal to look after."

"Doc Carney will help. There's a cat carrier in the hall closet."

The kitten finished the tuna, rubbed up against Christina, and purred. Christina scratched its tiny ears. It licked her hand and purred louder. Christina found the carrier, scooped up the kitten, and placed it inside. The kitten sat quietly on the ride to the vet's office.

Peering into the carrier, the receptionist asked, "So, who is this little cutie?"

"I'm Christina Mitchell, and I'm staying in the Benson condo this summer. I found this kitten outside their front door. I called Connie and she suggested I bring it here to see if it's chipped."

Dr. Carney was a middle-aged man with graying hair and a wide, gap-toothed smile. He shook Christina's hand and greeted her warmly.

"I hear you're Connie Benson's friend?"

"Yes," Christina replied. "They're in Maine this summer and I'm staying at their condo. I found this kitten today. It doesn't have a collar, but maybe it has a chip. I've never had a pet and I don't want one, but I don't think this kitten should be out wandering around. And it has something wrong with its paw. I thought it should get checked by a vet, and Connie said you might be able to find its owner."

"Well, let's take a look."

Dr. Carney reached in and gently lifted the kitten out of the carrier. He checked for a chip but didn't find one; then he gave the kitten a thorough examination. When he finished, the kitten wriggled free, jumped into Christina's arms, and cuddled against her.

"Well," Dr. Carney said, "*it* is a *she*. She's about twelve weeks old. She has ear mites and fleas, and she's very thin. We can get rid of the mites and fleas, and with a healthy diet she'll gain weight. As for the missing paw, it looks like she was born that way and it doesn't seem to cause her any pain. She has pads there, but the paw didn't fully form. She'll get around just fine. I think with a little medical treatment, good food, and some TLC, she'll grow up to be a beautiful cat. She seems to be pretty crazy about you. I think you two could become bosom buddies."

Bosom buddies. The vet's unintentionally poor choice of words blindsided Christina and she burst into tears.

"My goodness, Christina, what's wrong?" Dr. Carney helped her onto a bench. He placed the kitten back in the carrier as Christina sobbed uncontrollably.

Christina composed herself and gave the doctor a quick explanation that included her cancer diagnosis, the difficulties with treatment, and Marc leaving.

"Listen, Christina, my wife, Marie, is a fifteen-year breast cancer survivor. She'd be happy to talk with you. She understands what you're going through. As for this kitten, I think she would be good for you. Animals can be very therapeutic. There's no chip or collar, so she was probably abandoned, but she's friendly and well-behaved. I'd keep her here, but I'm full up with boarders and patients. I know you don't want a cat, but it would be a big help if you'd keep her while I try to find her a home."

"Who's going to want a kitten with only three paws?" Christina asked. "There are so many kittens; nobody is going to adopt one with a deformity."

"Oh, I bet there's someone who would take that cute little girl," Dr. Carney said. "And since she's being put up for adoption, we'll provide initial care at no charge. Could you just babysit for a while?"

Christina sniffled and accepted the tissues Dr. Carney

offered. "Well," she said, "I guess I could for a little while."

"Great! We'll get her fixed up this afternoon, and then if it's OK with you, Marie and I will stop by tonight with the kitten and we'll show you what to do. And if you like, you can talk with Marie about your health issues."

At seven p.m., Dr. Carney and his wife arrived with the kitten, cat supplies, a bottle of red wine, and a large Grotto pizza. Christina felt embarrassed about losing control in the doctor's office and wasn't sure she wanted to share her feelings with a stranger, but she was immediately at ease with Marie. They sat around the kitchen table and talked while enjoying the pizza and wine.

"I gave her a bath, treated her for the fleas and mites, and administered her shots," said Dr. Carney. "She's very healthy except for being underweight and a little anemic, but a good diet will take care of that. She's spunky and playful and doing really well."

"This kitten is a little furry ball of yellow sunshine," Marie said. "She'll make a nice companion for some lucky person. It's good of you to keep her until we find her owner or a new home. Now, let's talk about you. Jon tells me that you recently completed treatment for breast cancer. How are you feeling?"

After Christina described her diagnosis and treatment, Marie shared her own breast cancer experience and said that fifteen years later she was doing fine, with no recurrence.

"Well, that's certainly encouraging," said Christina.

"You should come to my cancer support group," Marie said. "You'll make some new friends and meet people who know how you feel."

Marie brought out a cat toy and had the kitten jumping and swatting at a cluster of feathers on a string. Christina found herself laughing at the kitten's antics. She couldn't remember the last time she had laughed out loud.

Dr. Carney gave Christina his business card with both home and cell phone numbers. "Call if you have any questions or concerns," he said.

As they left, Marie told Christina, "I'll pick you up at 6:30 on Monday evening for the meeting. And try to think of a name for that sweet little kitten."

After the Carneys left, Christina sat on the sofa to watch the news, and the kitten settled down beside her. Christina stroked her back. The kitten closed her eyes and purred.

"Marie is right," Christina said. "You do look like a little furry ball of yellow sunshine. I'll name you Sunny. Is that OK?" The kitten licked Christina's fingers. "I'll take that as a yes."

Later that night, when Christina went to bed, the kitten jumped up and cuddled against her right side. Christina never thought she'd allow a cat to sleep in bed with her. She drifted off to sleep, listening to Sunny's soothing purr. For the first time in weeks, she slept peacefully.

The next morning, Christina woke to find Sunny sleeping next to her with her head resting on the pillow. "You are unbelievably adorable," Christina whispered. As soon as she got out of bed, Sunny jumped up.

After they ate breakfast together, Christina got the cat toy and dangled the feathers. Sunny ran and jumped and swatted with her left paw, not at all affected by the missing right paw. "You've got a mean left hook, girlfriend," Christina said, laughing.

When she got tired, Sunny plopped down beside Christina. Christina touched the kitten's right front leg. "What a pair we are, Sunny girl. Did somebody throw you away because you're not perfect? That happened to me, too, so I know how it feels. Well, look, if you can get by with only three paws, I guess I can get along with a few scars."

Marie and Christina went to the cancer support group meeting, and afterward, Marie came in to visit the kitten. Sunny greeted them at the door and jumped into Christina's lap when the two women sat in the living room.

"Have you found her owner or a new home yet?" Christina asked.

"Not yet," Marie said. "But I think she's already found a home she likes."

"Oh, no. I really can't keep Sunny," Christina said.

"Sunny—that's a nice name. It fits her."

As the days passed, Christina realized she didn't feel so alone. She was sleeping better and feeling stronger. She started going out to lunch with Marie and her new friends from the cancer support group and taking walks on the beach every morning. When she returned, Sunny always greeted her at the door but made no attempt to escape.

Then, one day, Dr. Carney called. "I have a client who has a new kitten that needs a playmate. She might adopt Sunny.

Can she come over to meet her?"

Panic swept over Christina. She looked down at Sunny, who was curled up asleep on her lap. "Oh, she wouldn't want this gimpy kitten to go with a normal kitten, would she?"

"Maybe," Dr. Carney replied, "if they get along. They're both young and should adapt just fine."

"Well, Doc," Christina said, "I think we're kind of, you know, OK here." Christina could almost hear Dr. Carney's smile over the phone.

"Very good," he said. "You and Sunny just carry on then. I'll find Mrs. Lester another kitten."

Relief washed over Christina. "OK," she replied. "That's good."

"So you think you'd like to keep Sunny?"

"Yes, I guess so."

Dr. Carney laughed. "Kittens—they can steal your heart pretty darn quick."

The summer days flew by. Christina was taking a yoga class three times a week. She and Marie went on shopping excursions together to local farmers markets, antique shops, and the outlet stores. The kitten was eating well and filling out nicely. Christina felt a loving bond between them that she never would have believed could exist between a human and an animal. Christina knew that Sunny needed her, but she also realized that she needed Sunny.

On the last Saturday in August, Christina went to the

Carney house for their annual end-of-summer party.

"You'll get to meet our son, Dennis, today," said Marie. "He's on his way back home from a camp for inner city kids in the Pocono Mountains. He and his wife, Lauren, work there every summer."

A few minutes later, a handsome young man walked into the kitchen and gave Marie a big hug.

Marie kissed her son on the cheek and introduced Christina. "Christina is a professor at the University of Delaware in Newark. She spent the summer here in Rehoboth."

"Glad to meet you, Christina."

Marie looked around. "Where's Lauren?"

"Lauren is staying at camp a couple more days. She has our car and she'll drive back home on Monday. I caught a ride with Marty. He said he'd drop me off on the way if he could get some of your home cooking." Dennis turned to Christina. "Marty is a high school art teacher who works at the camp. Those kids are little Picassos when he gets done with them."

A tall, lanky man with thinning, blond hair entered the kitchen with a bouquet of flowers in one hand and a pet carrier in the other. He put the carrier down and handed Marie the flowers.

"Hi there, Mrs. C. Nice to see you again."

Marie hugged him. "Why, thank you for the beautiful flowers. Marty, this is our friend, Christina Mitchell. She spent the summer in Rehoboth, but she lives in Newark. She's a professor at the University of Delaware."

Marty took Christina's hand in both of his and smiled. "Well, hello, Professor Mitchell. I'm pleased to meet you."

His bright-blue eyes peered out from behind round, wire-rimmed glasses, projecting genuine warmth. He was not a tall, dark, gorgeous hunk like Marc, but it suddenly occurred to Christina that Marty's dimpled smile, sparkling eyes, and warm demeanor were every bit as appealing as Marc's chiseled features and six-pack abs. Perhaps even *more* appealing.

"What's in the carrier?" Marie asked, as she arranged the flowers in a vase.

"That," Marty explained, "is the camp cat—a chubby yellow tabby who showed up the day we arrived. We adopted him, or I should say, he adopted us. We named him Butterball. I call him BB for short. He's a character. He liked to hang out on my bed, so we did some male bonding, and, well, you know, I couldn't just leave my new pal behind. Guess I'm a soft touch when it comes to cats."

Marie smiled. "What a coincidence. Christina was adopted by a yellow cat this summer—a darling little female kitten. You're taking Sunny home with you, aren't you, Christina?"

Christina laughed. "Yes. I guess we're stuck with each other now."

Marty grinned. "Yeah, I know how that goes. BB decided he wanted to come home with me and I just couldn't say no."

Marie bent down and peered into the carrier. "Oh, he's handsome. You couldn't say no to a face like that!"

Marty smiled at Christina. "Hey, we should introduce our yellow cats. Maybe they'll fall in love."

Christina grinned. "Yes, maybe they will, Marty. Maybe they will."

Robin Hill-Page Glanden worked as a writer and in the entertainment industry in Philadelphia, New York, and Los Angeles for twenty years. Now back in Delaware, Robin is a freelance editor and writes magazine articles, fiction, nonfiction, and poetry. She performs music and spoken word with her husband, Kenny, and produces cabarets. Her short stories have been published in four anthologies, and three of those stories have won Delaware Press Association awards. Her poetry has been published in *Dreamstreets* magazine and in the *Delaware Bards Poetry Review* anthology. She is a regular contributor to *Mysterious Ways* and *Angels on Earth*, two of the *Guideposts* magazines. Robin is a fifteen-year breast cancer survivor and has served as a peer mentor with the Delaware Breast Cancer Coalition. She is a self-professed crazy cat lady who has been adopted by many cats and kittens through the years. She lives a happy, healthy, and grateful life with Kenny and their two fine felines, Teddy and Lucy.

Fireworks

by Katherine Melvin

As soon as she agreed, CJ Swift knew she'd regret letting her boyfriend talk her into having her eighty-year-old grandmother doggie sit for the weekend. It wasn't Mooshie, a Bernese mountain dog mix, she was worried about. It wasn't her grandmother Lou or her best friend, Millie, either. It was her house. Her very first house. Paid for with money she earned starring in *Baltimore Streets* with said boyfriend, Josh Brady.

Would her house survive the Fourth of July weekend?

Would Rehoboth Beach?

When she heard a car door slam, she peeked out the living room window. She gasped. Lou's hair, always colorful, was a star-spangled rainbow. *OMG.* So was Millie's. The Potomac Assisted Living Center, P-TALC, certainly went a long way toward catering to its "guests." Especially those two.

They looked like twins, dressed in their blue pedal pushers, red-white-and-blue striped T-shirts dotted with silver stars, and white sandals. She could just make out the blue-and-white sparkles that glittered in the red nail polish on their toes and fingernails.

Josh handed each lady a bag, then collected the luggage. As Millie turned to walk up the path, CJ saw what was written on the front of the bag. She flew out the door.

"No!"

"Granddaughter!" Lou opened her arms for a hug but was left hanging.

"No. No. *No.*"

Josh did the clueless-guy shrug, which included a sideways head thrust and dipped eyebrow. "What?" His lower lip hung down.

"You cannot possibly think it's OK to give two elderly ladies, in particular *these* elderly ladies, fireworks.

"They clobbered that thief in Baltimore last year, so we know they can take care of themselves." Josh, handsome in a young Tom Selleck sort of way, realized that was the wrong tack. "No worries, hon. Just sparklers." He made sure not to look at the grandmas, who were wise enough to keep quiet.

After an exhausting safety tour of the house that included locating the inside and outside water valves, the fire extinguisher, the electric panel, the alarm settings, emergency phone numbers, a list of food items prepared just for them, the vet's number, the emergency vet's number, pet food instructions, pet medicine doses, and potty instructions (for Mooshie, not them), CJ and Josh finally hugged the three girls—Lou, Millie, and Mooshie—goodbye and headed for the car.

"Oh," CJ called from the driveway, "keep Mooshie away from the cat next door. His name is Buttercup, but it should be Bulldog, and they don't get along."

"It'll be fine. What's the worst that can happen?" Josh asked as he locked them in.

Lou collapsed into an overstuffed chair, looking like Lily Tomlin's little Edith Ann sitting in her enormous rocker, only she was encompassed in flowers, stripes, and chintz. "I thought they'd never leave."

"Me, either." Millie stretched out on the cushy couch and yawned. "Nap time."

Mooshie, a black-and-white, long-haired mutt of epic proportions, sighed a huge doggie sigh and laid her head on her paws. *It's going to be a long weekend watching these two.*

Before they could finish their siesta, the doorbell rang. Mooshie woofed but without enthusiasm.

Lou struggled to sit, all the while crying a disoriented, "What? What? What?"

Millie opened the door. "Yes?"

"Well, hello there, ma'am. I'm Fred. Fred from next door."

The man was cute in an old-codger sort of way. She liked the way his blue eyes sparkled. Not much hair on top though. "Hello, Fred from next door. I'm Millie. What can I do for you?"

"It's more like what I can do for you. CJ mentioned you were here for the weekend. I'm having a barbeque tomorrow night and wondered if you young ladies would like to come. We'd be honored to have you."

"We?"

"Me and Buddy. He's down for the weekend visiting." He leaned forward and whispered, "Lives in a home over there in whatchamacallit."

"Don't know. What do you call it?"

After more than a few seconds, Fred said, "Gaithersburg."

"Doesn't everyone live in a home, Fred?"

"Not a regular home," he stuttered. "A *home*." He emphasized the word with finger quotes and raised eyebrows.

"Is he sane?"

"Right as rain."

Millie wasn't sure what rain had to do with sanity or being right for that matter. She closed the door in his face and went to tell Lou the news.

At dusk, Lou and Millie went outside in their pajamas and bare feet, something P-TALC frowned upon. CJ's small yard was homey, with a pergola-covered brick patio, a clay chiminea, and colorful annuals overflowing from planters of all sizes. There was a small, glass table, surrounded by cushioned chairs. Tucked away in the corner of the yard was a covered glider. The canvas overhang was taller than the fence.

Lou opened a box of sparklers. Together, they planted them in a circle on the grass away from the wooden fence.

"This is so much fun, Millie."

They giggled like schoolgirls committing a prank.

Mooshie paced and whined. *Oh dear, oh dear, this isn't such a good idea.* Since she couldn't speak human, she woofed and nudged the women with her cold, wet nose.

"Aren't you just a cutie-patootie." Lou rubbed Mooshie's silken ears.

Mooshie flopped over on her back, exposing her pink tummy. *Rub me, rub me. Maybe they'll stay out of trouble if they're busy taking care of me. Maybe I should eat grass and make myself throw up. That'd keep 'em entertained.*

Millie rubbed Mooshie's tummy. "Do you think there's something wrong with her?"

"Nah, she just wants attention. Don't you, old girl?"

Mooshie snorted doggie snot on Lou. *Old girl, my paw. At two, I'm still a youngster.*

Lou rummaged through the bag. "Where's that thingie with the long stick attached?"

"The thingie that shoots straight up with a big bang?"

"Yeah."

"In my room."

"I thought we both had one."

Millie shrugged. "I'll get mine."

"Look for matches."

While Millie was inside, Mooshie headed straight for Lou and started pushing her butt. *Gotta get this old coot in for the night, too.* Mooshie knew just what to do because she'd watched dogs herd sheep on the pet channel. Humans were no different. *Come on. Here we go—*

"Cut it out."

Mooshie persisted.

"Shoo."

Almost there. She had the one called Lou right by the door. *Shoot. The other one was back.* Mooshie sprawled on the patio, deflated. *Drat.*

Millie stuck the bottle rocket in the ground in the middle of the sparklers.

"This is gonna be good." Lou felt all bubbly, like she'd drunk a bottle of champagne. "Give me the matches."

"Couldn't find any."

"No one smokes anymore." Lou sounded disappointed. "In my day, everyone had matches."

"Or at least a lighter."

"Say, maybe the guys have some."

Millie fluttered her flowered gown. "Can we go dressed like this?"

"Why not? Didn't you say they're old?"

"Yep."

"Then they're blind." Lou headed to the gate.

Mooshie moaned and pulled herself up off the ground.

The house was dark, but a pair of pale green eyes stared at them through the bay window.

Mooshie's hair stood on end. *That cat is bad. Very scary.* She tried a woof, but it came out a whimper. *How embarrassing.* She was sure Buttercup snickered.

"Ring the doorbell," Lou ordered.

"There you are giving me orders again."

"Someone has to do it."

"Maybe they're already in bed, Lou."

"Nah." She reached around Millie and pushed the doorbell not once, but four times. When no one answered, Lou snorted.

"They're probably deaf, too."

Millie sniffed. "Do you smell that?"

Lou concentrated. "Borkum Riff. Cherry. One of 'ems smoking a pipe. They must be in the backyard. Come on, Millie." She bumped into the dog. "You, too, Mooshie."

As they approached, Lou realized the men still hadn't heard them. She drew Millie and Mooshie into a huddle. When she was certain they understood the plan, she started counting. "One, two, three."

"Boo!"

"Woof!"

The guys jumped.

Lou hooted.

"We didn't give you a heart attack, did we?" Millie asked.

"What are you doing out here? Shouldn't you two be in bed? It's …" Fred glanced at his Fitbit. "… almost eight-thirty."

Lou pulled herself up to her entire five-foot-one-inch height. "We're on vacation. What's it to you, anyway?"

"Well, your granddaughter asked—"

A man stepped out of the shadows. "Perhaps you'd like to join us." He gave Lou his arm and escorted her to the chair next to his.

"Well, aren't you a handsome one. You've still got hair."

"All white, I'm afraid."

"And a big old moustache."

The man couldn't help but smile as he slid his fingers over his 'stache.

Fred introduced them. "Lou, Millie, this is Buddy. Buddy, Lou and Millie."

Lou rubbed Mooshie's soft fur with her bare feet while she stared into the flames, thinking. "How'd you get the fire started?"

"The old-fashioned way. Two sticks rubbed together." Buddy displayed his "stick," made it click, and a flame appeared. "Actually, we used this modern contraption."

Lou grabbed for it.

"Nah, ah, ah." Fred pulled it away from her. "We're supposed to keep you ladies safe."

And out of trouble. Mooshie laid her large head across Lou's feet, just in case.

"Oh, fine."

Millie leaned forward to look at her friend, wondering what she was up to. Lou never gave in that easy.

The next morning, when only the birds were awake, Lou snuck out of the house and over to Fred's backyard. "Now where did he put that thing?" She looked around the fire pit, inside the gas grill cabinets, and under the chairs. Nothing.

"Looking for something?"

Buddy had scared the bejesus out of Lou, and if she were honest, a little pee, too. "What's the matter with you, old man?" She slapped his chest just like she'd watched Elaine do to Jerry Seinfeld.

He laughed. "I figured you might come looking for the lighter, so I took it inside last night."

"Oh, poop."

"Hey, how about an early morning walk on the beach?"

"Can I trust you?"

"Absolutely."

"Too bad."

"I've got coffee."

"High test?"

"Yes, ma'am."

"What are we waiting for?"

They stopped at CJ's house to let Mooshie out. She was agitated and barking like they were under attack.

"What's the matter, girl?" Buddy rubbed Mooshie's head.

"She won't leave my side. I had to listen to her snoring the entire night."

My snoring? Who's she kidding? The woman sounded like she was calling hogs all night.

It was only a matter of crossing the street, and they were on Rehoboth Beach. They sat on a bench and sipped their coffee.

"This is the life," Buddy said with a sigh. "I always thought I'd live at the beach and not—"

"In an old fuddy-duddy's home? Me too."

They watched the early morning walkers and listened to the waves roll ashore. A few seagulls pecked nearby, looking expectantly. When no bread was offered, they flew off.

"Too bad we can't all move in with Fred."

"Oh, he doesn't own that house. He's minding it for his son."

"And what are you doing?"

"Minding him."

"Well, isn't that a kick in the horse's hiney. Who's watching you?"

Mooshie barked. *Me.* She put a paw to her eye and then pointed at the old man, but the humans didn't get it. *Too bad.* She'd been working on that trick for weeks.

Lou jumped up. "I have an idea. Why don't you guys move into P-TALC? It's not so bad once you get used to it. You'd be fun!"

"How can you tell I'm fun?"

"I know things." Lou tapped her head. "There's mischief in those green eyes."

Buddy held up his hands in surrender. "You got me!"

They walked back to the house.

"Maybe I'll do just that, Lou." He gave her a peck on the cheek before she could protest.

Inside the house, Lou caught Millie and Fred snuggled up on the couch. "What's going on in here?"

"Just trying to remember what comes next," Fred said with a grin.

The four companions spent the Fourth of July morning at the beach until it became too hot and too crowded. They grabbed pizza from Grotto's and strolled Rehoboth Avenue, window gawking. Mooshie, under protest, remained at home.

"I'm beat," said Lou. "Let's go back."

"Me, too," Buddy said. "I've got a book I want to finish."

As Lou race-walked at an elderly pace, her phone rang. She stopped, swiped the button, and held it to her ear.

"Gramma?"

"Well, that's who you called, isn't it?"

"Is everything fine? Where are you? I hear people."

"Of course, you hear people. It's Rehoboth in the summer. They're everywhere."

Millie grabbed the phone. "CJ? Hey, it's Millie. Your grandmother is cranky and in need of a nap. The cottage is beautiful. Everything's fine. We'll see you tomorrow." She hit *End* before CJ could ask another question.

"I am not cranky."

"You are, too. You always get that way when you're tired."

"I am not tired! I get grouchy when you say I'm tired."

Twenty minutes later, Lou and Millie were home and sound asleep. The guys were at their house, reading with their eyes closed.

Lou and Millie arrived at the barbeque dressed in their Fourth of July finest, topped off with star-studded headbands. They had forced Mooshie to wear one, too. Her battery-powered stars twinkled in the dark, and she wasn't happy about it. Lou thought she saw Mooshie roll her eyes when they stuck it on her.

The fireworks were hidden in very large, very flowery, Vera Bradley totes.

"Presents?" Buddy reached for Lou's bag.

Lou pulled it back and sat it down beside her. She pushed it underneath the chair with her foot. "Sort of." She glanced away. "Hey! How about some of that good-smelling food?"

"Coming right up." Fred passed the plates around.

Millie smiled a false-toothy grin. "Fred, you sure know how to cook." She wiped barbeque sauce off her face and licked her fingers.

Lou burped. "Listen." She held up a bumpy finger when Millie started to speak. "Hear it?"

"The ocean. Amazing to be able to sit in your own back-yard and still hear the waves crashing." Buddy sighed with satisfaction. "Doesn't get any better than this."

The stars and a small flickering fire in the pit gave off the only light.

"Are we going across the street to the fireworks? Won't be long now." Fred stretched out his legs.

"Nah," Millie said. "Let's watch from the front porch away from the crowds."

Lou stood. "I have to pee."

Millie stared at her friend. "Thanks for the announcement."

"My pleasure."

"Don't let Buttercup out," Fred and Buddy called after her.

Please. Mooshie covered her eyes with her paws, awaiting disaster.

Millie removed the fireworks from their hiding place. "I think it's sparkler time." She stood up to sort through the mass of explosive devices. "Help me here, Fred."

Now Buttercup was not the color of butter, nor was he sweet like the flower. He was conniving. He knew if he closed his eyes, the old lady wouldn't see his beautiful black bulk scoot by her when she opened the door. Then he'd be able to pounce on that dumb dog before she knew what hit her.

"Eek," Lou squeaked. "Something soft brushed my ankle."

Fred and Buddy jumped up. "Buttercup!"

Oh, no. Mooshie sniffed, frantic. *Where are you?* She located her nemesis too late.

With amazing ease for such a large feline, Buttercup hefted his body into the air, extended all four sets of finely honed claws, and landed with a terrorizing shriek on Mooshie's back.

Yeeee-owwww. Mooshie jumped up, with the cat still attached. She shook, trying to eject the beast.

Buttercup growled and curled his claws in deeper. He was having a heck of a time. *Hee-haw!* He bounced from side to side. *Like riding a bronco, bareback.*

Get this thing off me! Mooshie barked and barked as she turned in circles.

The men ran after her, trying to grab the cat.

Millie stood beside the fire pit, fireworks in hand, mouth open.

Lou froze at the door, mesmerized by the spectacle.

Mooshie didn't mean to do it. She really didn't. In one final attempt to detach the cat, she jerked upright onto her hind legs, bumping into Millie. The cat did a slow, agonizing slide down her back, leaving four claw rows in her fur. Mooshie howled, then whimpered away.

As Millie fell, the fireworks flew out of her hands. The four friends watched as sparklers, missiles, bottle rockets, bangers, M80 firecrackers, and bombs fell into the fire.

"Take cover!" Buddy yelled.

The M80s were first to go off. From the other side of the fence, a neighbor yelled, "I'm calling the fire department." Several bottle rockets shot up. "And the police."

Look out! Mooshie bounded over to Lou, pushed her over, and lay on top of her.

"Get off!"

Woof. *No!* Mooshie refused to move. CJ had told her to protect Lou and protect Lou she would.

With booms and bangs, the flaming show flew out in all directions. The onlookers couldn't help but express "oohs" and "aahs." The larger, more potent fireworks flew across the fence on the other side, landing on top of CJ's glider. *Poof.* The canvas caught fire quicker than a snake fizzled. The sound of sirens grew. Buttercup yowled.

Mooshie howled. *Too loud. Too loud.*

Lou's cell phone rang. "Would someone get this dog off?" No one did. Mooshie licked her face. Lou squeezed her hand into her pocket and managed to get her phone out. "Hello?"

Firefighters flooded into CJ's backyard, hoses already flowing. The spray shot over the fence and drenched Millie, Lou, Buddy, Fred, and Mooshie.

"Gramma! Are those sirens?"

"Ma'am." A female police officer looked down at Lou.

"We've had a complaint about illegal fireworks."

"What?" CJ didn't need to be on speaker for those standing nearby to hear her scream, "Hand her the cell!"

The officer said, "Yes?" She listened. "Your house is fine. Your backyard, not so much." She moved the phone away from her ear. "Ma'am, we cannot take your grandmother to jail." She put the phone on speaker. "What happened here?"

"They fell out of my hands." Millie shook her wet hair, and tried to pat it flat before it started flipping up.

"The dog bumped her," Buddy offered. "Hard."

Fred added, "After Buttercup scratched her."

"Who's Buttercup?"

"The cat."

"A cat started all of this?"

"It all happened so fast." Lou wiggled out from beneath Mooshie.

The police officer stared at the four humans, the wet—and now stinky—dog, and the cat contentedly licking its paw. "I think everything's in hand now. The fire is out. The fence is history and you need a new glider. The people," she stressed, "are unhurt."

CJ's voice came through the speaker. "Who's staying with them until we get back? We'll be there as soon as we can."

"Not me." The officer arched an eyebrow.

Fred stepped forward. "Buddy and me."

"Yes, but who's chaperoning *them*?" CJ asked.

Mooshie barked. *Me.*

"OK, now that we have that all settled, I'll be going." The officer looked at the dog. "Maintain control. I don't want to come back out here."

Dried, dressed, and downing ice cream sundaes, the quartet sat on CJ's porch, watching the beach fireworks. Colorful sparkles lit up the sky.

"That's a show, all right." Lou put her bowl on the floor for Mooshie.

"Amen to that." Buddy yawned and stretched an arm around Lou's shoulders. "What a great night."

"Don't think I don't know what you're trying to pull, buster." Lou leaned on his shoulder.

Millie winked at Fred. "It's about to get better."

Mooshie finished off Lou's ice cream. Woof. *It can't get any better than this. Finally, I can relax.*

And Buttercup? He sat in the bay window of the house next door, in a Buddha pose, tail twitching, scratching a cat-sized hole in the screen, one claw at a time.

Katherine Melvin is a DC-based writer. Her Lou and Millie stories are inspired by the need to look old age in the face and laugh. Her seventy-pound dog KC—who her daughter swore would only weigh thirty-five pounds—lies faithfully by her side while she writes. Her short stories and articles have appeared in *Beach Days,* the 2014 *MWA Anthology, Today's Christian Women, Christianity Today,* and *Catholic Digest.* She's a proud member of the Maryland Writers' Association, which fosters writers of every level.

Zen

by Tara A. Elliott

A quick flick of the wrist
& all four feet scurry past concrete
until nails dig into Earth's soft leverage.
There is always this—the run,
the sleekness of muscle moving within her body,
the sheen of her coat in summer sun.
She knows nothing but the catch,
the hollow clatter of teeth against plastic.

She is Zen
& returns to me
to throw it again.

Tara A. Elliott's poems have appeared in *TAOS Journal of International Poetry & Art, The American Journal of Poetry,* and *Stirring,* among others. She is the founder and director of Salisbury's Poetry Week, co-chair of the Bay to Ocean Writers Conference, and the events coordinator of Eastern Shore Writers Association. In fall of 2018, she served as Poet-in-Residence for the Freeman Stage and was recently awarded a fellowship to the Virginia Center for the Creative Arts (VCCA). For more information, visit www.taraaelliott.com.

Courage

by Meg Ellacott

I t takes guts to be human. And it takes years of practice to grow afraid of life. Why is the ocean my safe place? My sanctuary? My refuge from the things in my life that never frightened me before and now do?

I am not afraid of spiders or snakes, crossing bridges, motorcycles, injections or germs, or heights. I am afraid of death, tsunamis and earthquakes, heavy snowstorms and ice, illness, car crashes, and the horror of another 9/11. So, too, I am becoming afraid of people, of being hurt. I am afraid of those I love the most hurting me the most, and I don't know how to become unafraid of their duplicity or their covert discounting of me.

Perhaps I am most afraid of becoming purposeless. So, I come to the ocean where gray, windswept boards are to be stepped upon, where the color and wind and light rinse my fears and loneliness clean.

Whatever happened to living without fear? I used to be ferociously determined, purposeful, taking on every black-diamond ski slope that came my way. Now, I'm afraid of blowing out my knee. I used to love being on the road, driving for ten hours at a clip. Now, my back hurts after two. I used to love to fly, but now I am convinced that something will go wrong with the plane, lightning will strike as did once before, guns on the aircraft, guns on the ground.

Fear: The anxiety, dread, or apprehension caused by the presence or anticipation of danger.

Last October, I was supposed to fly to Florida, only three hours from Philadelphia's International Airport to Tampa Bay. My sister had come all the way from New Jersey to take care of Sophie. A getaway for her. An in-home babysitter for my girl. But on that night, the night before I was supposed to leave for the airport, I couldn't catch my breath. My legs grew weak, and I had trouble falling and then staying asleep.

The next day, I drove the two hours to Philadelphia to stay overnight at an airport hotel for the following day's early morning flight. It was a murky, damp, and dirty hotel. Again, I couldn't sleep, and when I awoke from little to no sleep, my eyes gritty and my head pounding, terror washed over me. It had happened again: shortness of breath, a throat that seemed to snap shut, and legs that trembled while sun streamed in through dirty windows. A panic attack, I later learned.

I was supposed to be in the hot Floridian sunshine that day. I was supposed to be walking through pebbled beaches with my friends that day. But I wouldn't be.

I walked straight past that hotel's front desk, through dark, windowless passageways, back to the safety of my car. I drove back to Rehoboth, where I passed right by my street and my house and headed straight for the ocean. Once there, I was surrounded by everything familiar: quaint shops dotting Rehoboth's main avenue, the lighthouse circle, decorations for the Sea Witch Festival, the sound of crashing waves. I was calmed. I was safe.

I cried most of the way back to Rehoboth that day, the sky above impossibly blue. While driving, I called Becky, the friend whose Florida home my other friends and I were to visit. All six of them had made it there. I hadn't. It was to have been a celebration of us each turning sixty-five that year, in different months, on different days, nonetheless a festive milestone gathering.

On that call, made through tears of guilt and shame, I said I was sorry. I explained that I just could not get myself onto that plane. I explained that I realized I'd failed her. I knew how hard she'd worked planning the party and I'd let her down. Hell, I'd let myself down.

Sophie came into my life fearful. By that I mean she was timid, overly cautious, mistrusting; she'd somehow learned how to make herself appear invisible. So she wouldn't be a bother? So someone didn't have to love her? You can tell a fearful dog: wide eyes shifting left and right, tail tucked, backing away instead of coming forward.

I learned about her fears from the rescue league where I'd adopted other golden retrievers for more than two decades. Being a member of Golden Retriever Rescue, Education and Training (GRREAT), I called and expressed interest in adopting Sophie. Her write-up and her picture grabbed hold of me and wouldn't let go.

Turns out, Sophie had already been passed over by two other couples. She'd growled at one of them and backed away from the other after they'd pushed too hard. "Come here, pretty girl. C'mon Sophie, come to me." No. Dogs like Sophie need to come to you on their terms. Their rules. With warmth and with hope.

When I first met her, I'd had experience with other dogs who'd been fearful. Most of them had had some type of emotional, or even physical, issue. Sophie's foster parent from Maryland brought her to me. Sophie bounded out of the car and ignored me. I knew right away she was testing me. I knew she would have to learn to trust all over again. That would come. We made our way to the backyard and I let Sophie come to me when she was ready. On her own terms.

Seated on the steps of my deck, I'd watched her tentatively trot the grounds, stop and sniff the corners, and then run. She runs like a horse, I thought. She is enchanting, I thought.

I think I fell in love with her at that very moment—watching her fur and ears smooth back against her face, her long paws shoot out from beneath her as she raced with the wind. She would be the most beautiful, the most graceful, dog I'd ever had the privilege to adopt.

Every once in a while, she looked to her foster parent to make sure he was still there. That he hadn't abandoned her. Soon enough, she slowly approached me and sniffed my pant leg. I guess I passed the test. Her nose came under my hand, lifting it as if to say, pet me … I will trust you.

"I think she's grown overly attached to me," said Sophie's foster dad. "I've probably had her too long—six weeks and she's latched onto me like a forsaken pup."

"I can see that, Bob," I said. "She barely takes her eyes off you." After more play time and house exploring, I said to him, "Why don't we try letting her stay overnight with me and we'll see how it goes."

That night when Bob left us, Sophie became unnerved and anxious, so much so that, just for a moment, I thought I'd made a mistake. Perhaps I'd underestimated just how attached she'd become to him. Once Bob had closed the front door behind him, Sophie ran from the front door to the guest room window to the back door, and she did it over and over, letting out visceral yelps while racing from room to room. I stayed in my bedroom, giving her the space she needed to grieve, but then became worried about her level of panic, which seemed never ending.

I'd had fearful dogs before, but none had reacted like this when first taken from their fosters. I needed to distract her like a mom would do when her child was upset or afraid.

"C'mon Sophie, let's go in the car." Dead stop. She knew the word car. I opened the garage door and she raced to the car door and hopped into the back seat. We went to Concord, our local pet store. Once inside, we just walked around. I spoke to her, let her explore, let her feel as if she were in control. I introduced her to the folks I knew there, let her pick out a chew toy and take a treat from an employee's hand. Her tail slowly became untucked and began to wag, and that golden smile returned.

Sophie not only had emotional issues, but also physical ones. The physical issues had healed during her time in foster;

the emotional wounds were slower to resolve. Later, at home after our visit to Concord, she was quiet, seemingly contrite under my gaze.

I wondered about the life she'd lived before me. Had she suffered from cruelty, neglect, or disinterest by her "forever" parents before me? She had come into the rescue league in bad shape, with severely matted fur that had to be shaved. She'd had ear infections in both ears. There was evidence of tick-borne diseases her body's immune system had fought off. Sophie wasn't the only one who'd been through a lot recently.

Maggie, my third rescue from GRREAT, was eleven years old and slowing down. A lot. She had been diagnosed with glaucoma, and thus began the continual vet visits, the special eye drops, the lethargy, her sadness, and my sorrow. Not only was I consumed with worry over Maggie, but one of my friends was no longer sober, another one's career was making her sick (quite literally), and a close friend was going through a divorce. I was afraid bringing Sophie into my life during a time of upheaval wouldn't be good. For either of us. But I'd been on the "want to rescue" list for months and knew there would be others who would want to adopt Sophie. So, I had to go for it even if the timing wasn't right.

Turns out, Sophie came into my life just when I needed her most. Maggie's "glaucoma" turned out to be a brain tumor and I had to put her down (God, I hate saying those words). I thanked God every day that Sophie had come into my life when she did. That old adage became my mantra: Who, in fact, saved whom?

Sophie's fears and mistrust began melting away. She didn't instantly become my protector or jump on the bed for an ear scratch, but as I sat on the floor with her each day, trying to initiate play or lean in for kisses, she inevitably came a little closer. She began to approach me with a hand nuzzle or chase the yellow tennis ball. Before long, she rolled onto her back for belly rubs, paws straight up in the air, one of those submissive qualities of a dog that means I'm beginning to trust you.

She started to act as if this was her home, that she would protect it, and me, and that her voice would be heard. She soon barked at everyone who passed the house, her bark becoming louder if they came on the property, and if they rang the doorbell, she let loose with ear-piercing yelps and growls. So much so that I've gotten rid of my costly alarm system. So much so that I've watched many a mailman or UPS delivery guy run from my front door.

Her slow start gathered steam as those first few days bled into months and as cold, wintry, wind-driven days switched over to warm, moonlit nights. Somehow, my nearly forgotten frustrations of those first few days shifted to wonder. I began to feel like new parents must as they eagerly await their child's hitting another milestone.

It is our mission when rescuing these creatures to rehabilitate, to bring them back to who they were before drastic change or sadness, to return these dogs to their normal state of being. And it was happening again, just as it had with the others I'd saved: that transformation.

Sophie became less territorial with her toys when other dogs came around. She was actually retrieving the ball, not just fetching it, falling into a rhythm with me, a consistency she could depend upon. It's something that's hard to describe. When that bond comes, how magical it is. How in sync you are with each another. That bond, sometimes coming overnight, sometimes happening in only a few days, and sometimes occurring only after months of painstaking patience and hard work.

Sophie now seems to feel secure, as if this is her forever home; I am hers and she is mine. As if it has been that way all along. I've seen these transformations before in each of the golden retrievers I've adopted but none as radical, nor fast, nor deep, as Sophie's. And watching these changes, when a dog returns to that happy, loving, confident dog she was prior to trauma, has led me to feel like my own worldview has evolved.

It's made me think that if a dog can leave her fears behind and change, maybe it's possible for humans like me to transform, too.

Day in and day out, as Sophie and I mosey along Rehoboth's weather-beaten boardwalk with the sound of seagulls squawking above, I think maybe, on one of those days, I'll have a transformation of my own. I'll leave my fears behind. I'll have the guts to climb aboard that plane and fly off to Florida.

Born and raised on Long Island, New York, Meg Ellacott spent most of her adult life in the Washington, DC, area and moved to Rehoboth Beach, Delaware, in 2007. She has had articles published in trade magazines, has crafted press releases, and has written promotional copy for animal rescues and other nonprofits. She is a board member of the Rehoboth Beach Writers Guild, has studied creative writing, and in 2013 published a true-crime book about a tragedy in Lewes, Delaware, *Ultimate Betrayal: The Sex Abuse Case Against Dr. Earl Bradley*. She has been published in two other anthologies.

Meg shares her home with Sophie, her golden retriever/ Great Pyrenees mix and is currently working on her next book titled *Rescued*, a memoir about life, love, and how animal rescue connects us all.

Beautiful Disaster

by Adrianne C. Lasker

*D*isaster came into my life the day I left for my home in Rehoboth Beach, Delaware, September 5, 2005.

Fresh from a nasty breakup, I came to the stark realization that I wouldn't be hearing the organ playing Wagner's wedding song any time soon. U-Haul bulging with my stuff, which had been hastily and haphazardly shoved in that morning, I couldn't get out of that Florida town fast enough. I wanted to become Dorothy from *The Wizard of Oz* so I could click my heels together and be home on the sands of Rehoboth Beach *right now*. Stopping at Starbucks to fuel the drive, I spotted a poster in the window:

Please Help
Save This Dog
Home Needed
No Time Left

I didn't need to read the rest to know the fate of this shelter animal.

Two soulful black eyes stared into my soul. One broken

ear (the other standing at attention) and a pink nose scraped raw, completed the package. Quickly grabbing my grande, I asked Hilda (aka Google Maps) to take me to: Abandoned Pet Rescue, 1874 Northwood Drive, Ft. Lauderdale, Florida.

A pothole-filled road led to a once brightly painted, now chipped and worn, wood frame house. The old U-Haul shivered and moaned as we made our way to the parking space out front. I heard the barks, howls, and pleading yelps before I even opened the door. My mind filled with all the practical reasons I should not be here, but my heart yanked me out of the truck.

I was greeted at the door by an effervescent, disheveled lady wearing a stained "Rescue is My Favorite Breed" T-shirt, bright-pink muck boots, and a name tag that read "Sandra." She smiled a big welcome.

"Hurricane Katrina was a Category 5 hurricane," Sandra explained. "Two hundred fifty thousand animals of all kinds were stranded on rooftops, hung onto logs in the flood waters, huddled in abandoned homes, or were rescued from drowning while swimming for their lives."

We walked by the rows of cages. Some dogs were barking, some were spinning wildly for attention, and others seemed to know that they would be passed by once again. Thin rays of sunshine squeezing through the high windows appeared to send a sliver of hope for a brighter day.

"We have lots of puppies and young dogs you will just love," Sandra babbled in a stressed-out voice.

"No. This is the one I came for." I pulled the crunched poster out to show her.

There was a slight pause, a raised eyebrow, and a questioning look.

"Oh, OK. Most people don't want adult pit bulls, they want puppies."

While I sat in the greeting room, Sandra brought in a rambunctious, fluffy, brown-and-white pup. Jumping, tail on overdrive, panting madly, bounding to and fro, this little guy reminded me of the Mad Hatter in *Alice in Wonderland.*

"We sent one of our volunteers to the overflow kennels out back to find the dog you requested," she said. "It might take a few minutes, so I thought I would bring Jingles to keep you company while you wait."

A ploy? Possibly.

After a while, another volunteer came in, pulling a leash that bent around the door jamb. I held my breath. Then, as he tugged the leash gently, a pink scraped nose and two familiar black eyes appeared. The rest of her pitiful, brindled body emerged, waves of ribs jutting out, nipples hanging almost to the floor, tail wrapped under boney hindquarters. This, by far, was the sorriest, most emaciated mutt I had ever seen. My heart constricted in my chest.

I started to cry. Softly at first, then a full-blown, ugly cry that promised to be unrelenting. Looking through the watershed of tears, I saw the dog's sad face rise slowly, all the way up, and her tail, too, trepidation replaced with an inner mission.

Prancing over with purpose, she put her gentle paws on my knees and began licking my tears away. I took her kind, scarred face in my hands, and, forehead to forehead, told her, "Oh, my God! You are just one lost disaster. Just like me." *Disaster.*

A human arm reached into my cage. Afraid and cold, I clung to the corner.

"C'mon old girl, someone wants to see you. Now be good because an ugly dog like you ain't gonna get many chances for a new life."

My paws were stiff and sore on the concrete surface. I thought, *Are my humans coming back for me and my pups?* It had been so long since the flood waters chased my people away. Men in yellow vests rescued me and my pups from the second floor of our home, and we ended up here. So many humans came looking for their pets, but not mine. My pups were all taken away, though, each cuddled by small humans and their families. Did my people, whom I loved and protected, finally find me? Is that where I was being taken?"

Head down, feeling scared and unsure, I slowly poked my head around the door. What I found was a sad-looking human with long, straggly, red hair, hunched over, making strange sounds. *Oh, my! What was this?*

As soon as I looked into her eyes, my protective drive kicked in. *This one needs help.* Quickly going to her, I jumped up, front paws on her knees, and licked the salty water flowing from her face. Nuzzling my way into her arms, I knew I had found a home. I was needed here.

On the way out to the U-Haul, papers signed, adoption fee

paid, I stopped short. As I eyed the bulging vehicle, realization hit: Where would this disaster sit? There was no room for even a pen. "Disaster, look at all this. Something has to go." Opening the passenger door ever so slowly, I reached for the boxes piled on the front seat and set them on the ground.

The boxes contained blankets, pillows, sheets, and a horrid bedspread. All items had been purchased on our trip to Bed, Bath and Beyond when my now ex-fiancé and I had been setting up our forever fantasy home. I had been starry-eyed in love. Pulling out the dreadful gray-and-navy bedspread, the one he had wanted, I remembered that day and tears welled up. Again.

Our cart had been overflowing with nesting items unclaimed from our bridal-shower registry. I had wanted the colorful, geometric, abstract, Piet Mondrian bedding. He had scrunched up his face in disapproval. Disappointing, but love is about compromise, right?

Thinking back to those items in the cart, I recalled lamps with dreary, black shades; dusty, muted-mauve towels; and a black—yes, black—plastic soap dispenser, all picked by him. Compromise? The only item he acquiesced to was the red, Micky and Minnie, bride and groom pillows that declared, "and they lived happily ever after."

But that didn't happen, did it? Sitting in the grass, my furry partner by my side, I read the scrawled words on the next box: iron, towels, Tide, tablecloths. "When in the world was the last time I ironed?" Disaster tilted her head left, then right. I never liked the towels, or any of this, actually. Why did I agree with everything? I had been so weak. Huh! All this could go to good use at this shelter. "We won't need these,

Disaster; let's leave them here for your friends to cuddle with."
A muzzle poked through my arm. Agreement noted.

We hit the road, much lighter in many ways. I thought
about the iceberg floating away from me now. How could I
have missed the signs? Another life lesson learned the hard
way: Beware the tip of the iceberg, for it is only a small
part of the unseen hazard. I should have taken a deep dive
below the surface before accepting that diamond ring. What
a controlling mess of a man! Well, as far as I am concerned,
by leaving him, and adopting my beautiful Disaster, I have
certainly traded up.

The rest of the trip home consisted of long rants and life's
confessions to my furry copilot, while songs blasted from the
radio. Some songs brought more tears, while others made me
sing out, in full-throttle voice, From Kelly Clarkson's "Since
You've Been Gone" and Green Day's "Boulevard of Broken
Dreams" to Mariah Carey's "Shake it Off," I conveyed the ex-
cruciating pain or the hallelujah elation of my erratic feelings.

Disaster seemed to enjoy most of it and smiled a wide,
pit-bull smile while her tail thumped on the seat. She just
knew when to make me laugh by cocking her head in that
quirky way. Sometimes, she just retreated to the floor. I don't
think she is fond of Mariah Carey.

We are home. October is one of the best times in Rehoboth
Beach. Summer crowds have gone, and people drive down
on weekends to catch the last rays of autumn sunshine, walk
on the boardwalk, and fill up on the last tastes of the season.
Kites fly high, sunbathers top off their tan, and beach disciples

check into their favorite cozy inns before they close for the winter. Surf anglers dot the beach, seeking places with the fewest bathers and surfers. Beach cottage gardens still bloom with asters, sedums, and chrysanthemums, the colors of fall drawing butterflies and birds that are reluctant to leave this sandy haven before their long journeys to winter destinations.

Disaster and I have settled in just fine. At first, she was fearful of the water, especially the waves chasing her paws at the surf's edge. But she quickly became crazy about the sand. The first time her toes touched the fine grains, she seemed to do a ballerina dance—up on tippy-toe, slowly prancing and dancing, then flying down the beach for no good reason other than the sheer joy of it. After digging holes so deep her snout burrowed in up to her ears, she emerged, face covered in wet sand, with that full, pit-bull smile.

This is the time of year dogs can go free on the Rehoboth beach, and they seem to explode with exuberance. Greeting, rolling, romping, and racing, the dogs fill the whole sandy shore with their wet and wild canine antics.

I love to watch Aster play. Yes, I shortened her name to that of a beautiful flower, because she was now in full bloom.

The water laps about my feet, and I think of the past four years. Trying to be someone I wasn't, compromising myself for someone else, being blind and inconsiderate of my own feelings, wants, and desires. Trying to love someone who rebuffed the love I offered.

We are home now. No icebergs here; this is Rehoboth Beach. I am happy to spend life in this magical village, along with four, faithful, sandy paws of love, so blessed to have found and rescued this trusting, faithful, forgiving, and loving pooch from that sad and lonely cage. Aster now owns my heart.

Well, I think she is OK now. During that long trip, I watched my broken, lost human plunge into despair then soar to feverish heights, while her heart tried to mend. I showered her with love, made her laugh, nuzzled her arm, curled up against her side, and kissed her tears away. She seems happy here in this beautiful village of friendly, laughing humans. I am completely devoted to her and so happy that I rescued her from such sadness. My heart is hers.

Adrianne C. Lasker spent most of her career in marketing, public relations, and policy development. She is a champion of dog rescue and adoption, and *Sandy Paws* allowed her to share this passion with readers. She is a lifelong lover of books, the creative process, and the ability of authors to send readers on thrilling journeys. Her secret dream had been to try her hand at fiction, and it has now become a reality with this first published piece. She says she was nervous to press the *Send* button, but glad she did. Bailey (2005-2019) was the inspiration for this story.

Sometimes You Just Have to Dive In

by Lonn Braender

I sighed as I approached my townhouse. There, in the window, sat Paddy, tail wagging and head bobbing in time to my steps. Sometimes I wish he were, but no, Paddy is not my dog. He's my ten-pound, sable cat with iridescent emerald eyes.

Now that the tourists have gone home, the place to meet people in Rehoboth is the beach at sunrise. It's like MeetUp.com with one exception: you either bring a dog or you meet someone who has a dog. The problem is Michael doesn't have a dog and neither do I.

Michael is this really nice guy I've been lusting over. He's handsome, with an enchanting smile, which he gives away freely. I've been watching him all summer but never got the nerve to say more than hello. Besides, he's always with someone—someone way better looking or in way better shape than me.

Michael and I chatted briefly once at Aqua Grill; actually, I said "excuse me" as I squeezed past him. But last week I said to my cat, "no more" and went to the beach to meet him. But just like at Aqua Grill, he was with a hunky guy. This time it was EJ with his perfect dachshund.

Of course, I have a cat. But he's not your typical feline. I'm pretty sure Paddy thinks he's a dog, and a big dog at that. For example, I live in this older townhouse development on the forgotten mile. There's a spacious lawn surrounded by our five buildings. It's picturesque and peaceful, and the residents spend a lot of time out on the lawn. Many of my neighbors have dogs and they all play on the lawn, but not one will come anywhere near my place. The dogs keep a wide berth, especially if the sliding glass doors are open. As soon as they get close, my cat makes an ungodly sound and they bolt.

You're probably thinking Paddy hisses. Nope. Paddy doesn't hiss or meow. In fact, Paddy has never meowed in his life. He makes guttural noises that sound like gears grinding in my old '67 VW beetle. And, if a dog happens to pass by, Paddy prances in front of the doors like a caged bull ready to strike. I thought cats kept their distance from dogs. Not Paddy. He'd take on any of them, big or small.

Two years ago, the young couple who lived next door with their ginormous shepherd (it must have weighed a hundred pounds) stopped by to chat. We sat on my patio, the shepherd on the ground next to them. All of a sudden, Paddy came barreling across the living room toward us. The noise emanating from this ten-pound feline sounded like a forty-ton freight train. We all looked up just as Paddy launched himself into the screen door. The dog sprang straight up like a cat and shot off. He took off so fast my neighbor ended up with a wrenched shoulder and a leash with an empty collar. It took them an hour to bring that dog home. After that, the dog refused to walk by my house; he couldn't even be dragged past my patio.

When not scaring the crap out of dogs, you'd think Paddy might meow, especially as I scrape food out of a can into his bowl. Again, no. From the beginning, he refused to eat cat food. I've tried them all and the food will sit there until it petrifies; he won't even try it. Guess what he will eat? Yep, dog food.

When Paddy was young, a friend kitten-sat for me. He brought his dog with him for the day. Well, little Paddy made the dog run and hide, and then ate the dog's food. Eventually the dog came out and they started playing like two dogs. But Paddy has eaten nothing but dog food ever since.

The only time Paddy acts like a cat is at bedtime. He curls up in a ball at the back of my knees and purrs. And purrs. And purrs. The damned thing is a broken record (but I find it comforting).

My friends mock Paddy because of his vocals and the dog thing, but they secretly like him. Paddy's a lot like me—different. So what if he growls (or even moos, as he sometimes does) instead of meows? Who cares if he chases dogs instead of being chased by them? Paddy is just a different kind of cat, and I love him.

I woke early the following morning but not because the sun was streaming in or the birds were extra loud. No, I had four paws standing on my chest, a whisker-flanked wet nose pressed against mine, and a rumbling noise thundering in my ears.

"What?" Why I keep talking to a cat is beyond me. It's not like either of us understand a single noise the other makes.

"OK, I'm up. Let's see what's got you all upset." I stretched, but the cat didn't get off me, so I picked him up and put him on the floor. Paddy started pacing, then headed downstairs, but he didn't race to the kitchen where his bowls were. Instead, he went to the front door, paced, and rumbled.

Paddy is not an outdoor cat. Not that he couldn't take care of himself; I'm sure he could. He's the most confident cat I've ever met. Hell, he's more confident than most people I know, especially me. But I'd worry about him being hit by a car or something.

Leaving him to pace, I went to the kitchen and started coffee. I put down a bowl of his favorite dog chow and whistled for him. He answered with an even louder noise, a cross between the rumble and a moo, followed by clicking. When I stepped back into the hall, Paddy was up on his hind legs, pawing at the doorknob.

"What?"

Rumble-moo.

"Since when do you rumble?" I laughed, but he didn't. Instead, he started batting the doorknob. Next, he scratched at the door jam. I pulled him away, not wanting claw marks in my door, but he went right back at it. So, I opened the door, knowing the screen door would hold him. He jumped at the handle. This was a first, so I did the only thing I could think of. I found a rope, tied it to his collar, and opened the door.

I've heard people walk cats, but I've never seen anyone do it. Yet there I was, early morning, walking a cat. He didn't sniff around or study the landscape. Paddy acted like this was an everyday event and walked right to the parking lot. The cat didn't scurry out, he held his shoulders strong, his tail perfectly straight, without a single twitch, and he never turned his head. He marched straight on, pulling me with him.

We didn't go far. He prowled the immediate area, stared down a squirrel, and we were back at our door before anyone saw us. Thank God, because my neighbors already think I'm odd. What would they say if they saw me walking my cat?

Well, that wasn't the end of walking, Paddy made a fuss at the door again the next two mornings. On Thursday, after work, I gave in and stopped at the pet store. I bought a harness, thinking it would be more secure then a collar, and a retractable leash—both pink. If I was about to make a fool of myself, might as well do it with style. While there, I bought some discounted dog food—screw him.

As the clerk rung up my purchases, she asked, "Do your cat and dog get along? Did you get them when both were babies?"

"I just have a cat. He'll only eat dog food." I'm not sure why, but I burned with embarrassment.

"How odd." She sneered.

Sure, it was odd, Paddy was odd, but so was I. So, I said loud enough for everyone to hear, "I celebrate his diversity. It's not a choice, you know." I puffed out my chest, picked up the bag, and tried to march out. But as is my life, the bag split and six cans scattered on the floor, rolling off in all directions. It's hard to look righteous when you're chasing discount beef stew across the store. Nevertheless, that gave me an idea, one I hoped wasn't too terrible.

On Saturday, I surprised Paddy by waking before him, before dawn. He seemed confused and stayed curled up, watching me dress. I smiled, then did what I always do—I talked to him.

"Paddy, my friend, we're going to do something crazy today. Get up and put on your best fur coat." I rubbed his cheek; he really likes that.

He stretched but still didn't get up.

"Come on, pal, we've places to go." I jogged down to the kitchen, put some dog food in his bowl, and made coffee. Eventually, he came down, looking at me skeptically.

"You're gonna wish you'd eaten your breakfast," I said.

Paddy grunted. I'm not sure if him meowing, like a normal cat, would have given me any more insight.

Paddy followed me to the bathroom and watched me shave. I talked to him, as I usually do. If someone heard me, they'd think me crazy, having a conversation like that with a cat.

When I was ready, I sat on the floor and waited for him to approach. He cocked his head and narrowed his eyes as he advanced. When he was close, I grabbed him and sat him on my lap. Getting the harness on him was easier than I imagined. I thought we'd tussle over it, but he let me slip it on and sniffed the collar that I took off. I think he understood because as soon as I snapped the harness in place, he bolted for the door. I swear Paddy was a dog in a previous life.

Since it was the first time, and I didn't know if Paddy could walk a full mile, we drove to the beach. I was nervous about this but in for a penny, in for a pound. I parked, grabbed Paddy, and off we went. I carried him to the boardwalk, which was an effort. That cat was wide-eyed and excited, simultaneously purring and mooing.

I put him down near the sand. He looked around so fast I thought his head would spin off. He didn't know what to look at first, until he heard a bark. Then his attention was laser-focused on the beach. He didn't dash off, he took definite steps, one at a time, until we reached the sand. When his front paw hit the sand, he stopped and looked down, until he heard another bark. There, about a hundred yards away, were two dogs chasing a ball and splashing in the surf.

This time, Paddy didn't hesitate, he took off like a rocket, only to be jerked back when he reached the end of the leash line. That didn't stop him; he tugged and tugged until I yanked him back to my side.

"Hey, listen." I knelt and spoke in his ear. "Don't go scaring off the other dogs. We're here to make friends, not chase everyone off the beach. OK?"

Paddy grunted. What did that mean?

Thank God I'd bought the retractable leash. I reeled it back and kept him close. There were probably a dozen people and four dogs down near where Rehoboth Beach ends and Dewey begins. I noticed that none of the dogs were on a leash, and that's when I realized the error in my plan. There was no way Paddy would be able to keep a pack of dogs at bay. One, probably two, sure. But four? No way, and other than the lifeguard chair, there was no place for a cat to run to safety.

I stopped and was about to turn around when I saw his raven-black hair. Michael was walking toward me, talking with someone and tossing a ball to a small dog. God, even in a bulky sweatshirt, he was gorgeous. As much as I wanted to say hello, I couldn't, so I turned to leave.

"What the hell is that?"

Once again, EJ arrives just in time to ruin my day. Damn it! He was laughing at Paddy, who was still focused on the dogs down by the surf and hadn't noticed EJ's dachshund yet.

"You brought a stupid cat? The sign up there says dogs allowed, not cats and dogs."

I'm about to flip him off when his perfect little dachshund starts yapping like a squeaky toy.

If I hadn't had Paddy with me, I would have looked for storm clouds, but I knew where that thunder noise emanated from, so I started retracting the leash—fast. Just as EJ's hot-dog started his attack, the rumble turned into a roar, and the showdown was on. I yanked the leash just as Paddy sprang, pulling him back to the sand with a jerk, but not before EJ's perfect dachshund yelped, turned, and charged up the beach. I'm not sure whether Paddy swiped the dog's nose or just scared the hell out of him, but that dog was gone.

"Dude, what the hell?" EJ looked from me to his retreating dog.

"Dude, teach your dog some manners." I straightened my shoulders, held my head high, and walked away with my cat.

I walked slow for a few steps, then stopped and picked up Paddy. I was about to continue the retreat when someone called my name. I assumed it was EJ, but when I looked up, Michael was waving at me. I gave a quick wave back but didn't move.

Michael said something to the guy next to him and pointed.

I turned beet red. This was the worst idea I'd ever had, and I've had some stupid ideas. I wanted to leave, but Michael had already started jogging toward me.

"Shane, hi. I've never seen a cat on a leash before."

"Hi, Michael." I cocked my head a bit. "How do you know my name?"

"John, the bartender from Aqua Grill told me." Michael smiled. "I can't believe your cat likes the beach."

"Well, to be honest, it's his first time." I put Paddy down.

"He's beautiful. Can I pet him?"

"Of course." I was sweating. "Paddy, this is Michael."

Michael squatted and reached over. As soon as he touched Paddy's head, the cat flopped over and offered his belly for a rub.

"Paddy! How rude. You just met Michael."

Michael laughed, but I shook my head. Michael rubbed Paddy's belly and the cat started purring. Really? There are dogs just yards away and this cat is purring?

"Paddy is a cute name." Michael stood and smiled. "So is Shane."

My heart skipped a beat and I turned away, grinning.

"John warned me you were shy."

I turned even redder and couldn't speak.

"Paddy is such a good cat." Michael touched my arm.

"Not always; as you saw, he scared the fur off EJ's dachshund." I looked around, EJ was nowhere in sight.

"Ha!" Michael bellowed. "That yappy thing? Good. He

deserved it. That dog snapped at me when I tried to pet it. EJ hasn't trained it at all. He uses the poor thing to pick up guys. Someone told him little dogs are date magnets, so he bought that beast and struts around like he's a god."

My head jerked up. "Aren't you dating him?"

"Me? Yuk." Michael leaned back down to pet Paddy, who was now rubbing against his ankles.

"But I saw you two on the beach last week." My eyes went wide; I had just given myself away.

Michael grinned at me. "He was working that dog, but I'm not stupid. Anyone who gets a dog just to pick up guys is desperate."

I gulped, audibly.

"What?"

"Well, I brought Paddy because I don't have a dog." I looked away again.

"You didn't." Michael laughed, but he squeezed my arm again.

"Yeah, I did."

"That is too funny. I love it."

"You don't think I'm as stupid as EJ?"

"You obviously didn't just go get Paddy. I don't think EJ has even given his dog a name."

"I've had Paddy since he was a kitten, but he's not your average cat. He's not afraid of dogs. In fact, dogs are scared to death of Paddy."

"You have a nice smile."

I blushed and shrugged.

"It's so cute how you blush. I'd have guessed someone with balls enough to bring his cat to the beach would be all macho and crap."

"Me? Macho?" I laughed. "I can't even spell *macho*, but Paddy is macho enough for us both."

I noticed the guy Michael had been talking with was coming our way with his dog.

"Hey, I have a cat here," I called and pulled the leash tight.

"So I see." He approached and held out his hand. "You must be Shane."

I shook his hand. "Do I know you?"

"Kyle, and we've not met, but I was with Michael when John told him about you."

"Really? Why?" John wasn't a close friend. He'd been a bartender at Aqua Grill for a few years and we'd gotten to know each other, somewhat. He always remembered my name and sometimes forgot to add a drink to my tab.

"He's a would-be matchmaker," Kyle said.

I noticed his dog was staring at Paddy. "He's not your usual cat. He thinks he's a dog. He just chased EJ's dog down the beach."

"That's no dog; it's a mop-head with a temper. My dog's cool, even with cats." Kyle looked at the two animals, his was standing a few feet away, eyes glued to Paddy, but his tail was wagging. Kyle didn't seem concerned.

"You don't understand; he thinks he's top dog. He even barks instead of meowing."

Kyle knelt and held out a hand, and damn if the cat didn't roll on to his back, even with a dog not five feet away. "What's his name?"

"Paddy," Michael told him. "He's a sweetheart."

Kyle stood and turned to call his dog. "Skippers, come, but go easy; Paddy's a cat."

Kyle's dog sniffed, looked around, and eased his way into the group. Paddy did the same, sniffing the air and eying the dog warily. The two animals inched toward each other, and as if on cue, both lowered their chests to the sand while keeping their hind quarters up and ready to pounce. It was Paddy who pounced first, yanking the leash from my hand. The two pets didn't go far, chasing each other around, weaving in and out of our legs.

I grabbed the leash on one pass, jolting Paddy to a stop. Skipper stopped short, as soon as he realized he wasn't being chased.

"Let Paddy go; he'll be fine," Michael said.

Against my better judgment, I released him and said, "I have no idea if I'll ever catch him."

Freed from his tether and caught off guard, Paddy ran toward the surf with Skipper close on his tail.

"Damn!" I was about to tear after my cat, but Kyle stopped me.

"I'll get him."

Kyle took a tennis ball from his pocket, called out his dog's name and threw the ball. The chase stopped immediately. Skipper caught sight of the ball and bolted after it. Paddy saw the dog take off and turned to follow. The dog caught the ball and ran directly back to Kyle, dropping it at his feet, forgetting all about the cat he'd just been chasing.

But Paddy was not to be forgotten. He swooped in, laid his fangs into the ball, and took off. Skipper looked at Kyle and then at a sprinting Paddy. He barked once.

Kyle laughed and said, "It's your ball; go get it."

The dog took off fast, but he didn't have to go far. The ball was big for a cat's mouth, and so Paddy dropped it a few yards away. Skipper dashed in, nabbed the ball, and ran back to Kyle. And just as he dropped it at Kyle's feet, Paddy bounded in and stole it again.

"I can't believe it." I shook my head. "I was afraid Paddy would chase all the dogs away."

"Really?" Kyle asked.

I told Kyle the shepherd story; he laughed.

"Hey, let's try something." Michael grinned, and his smile melted my heart.

The next time Skipper brought the ball back, Michael scooped it up before Paddy could grab it. He leaned back and threw the ball. The dog bolted, as did the cat, only Paddy stopped when he got to the water. Skipper dove in after the ball.

They did that twice, and each time, Paddy stopped at the water's edge. I could see the cat's frustration and then, suddenly, on the third throw, in he went, chasing the dog. Paddy didn't get the ball, but he did get wet, which was a first, and maybe a last because the cat came running right back to me. He was done. He was panting and shaking and licking his fur. I picked him up.

Kyle's dog came back, this time dropping the ball far enough away so no one could pick it up.

"Well, I guess I should get Paddy home and dried off." I gave a sad smile.

"When will I see you again?" Michael asked.

"I could bring Paddy again tomorrow ..."

"I was thinking, maybe later on today—sans cat."

"It sounds like what you two really need to do is stop by Aqua Grill and thank John," said Kyle.

Michael smiled and gazed me. "For sure."

I started to smile and then remembered. "But they don't open until four."

"Let's not worry about that." Michael leaned over, stroked Paddy once and kissed me on the cheek.

Lonn Braender is a Jersey-born artist, printer, business-man, entrepreneur, and writer. He was a painter of landscapes and seascapes for more than twenty-five years, but due to life changes he found an alternative creative outlet—writing, which has become his passion. Lonn has written dozens of works of varying lengths. His first short story, which won a judge's award, was published in the 2016 anthology *Beach Nights*. Subsequently, he has been published in the 2017 anthology *Beach Life* and the 2018 anthology *Beach Love.* His story for the 2018 anthology, *Beach Fun,* won third place. All were published by Cat & Mouse Press. Lonn lives in Bucks County, Pennsylvania, with his muse and their two sable kittens: Pippin and Paddy.

The Case of the Lost Lhasa

by Doug Harrell

*L*ucy, where are you?" Colin, tall, dark, and frantic, was searching his beach rental for any sign of his little dog. He had just woken and had been startled not to find her at his feet. He dashed outside calling her name, only to realize he was dressed in the plaid boxers and ripped T-shirt he had slept in. Sheepishly slinking back inside, he tossed on shorts and sneakers, grabbed his keys, and ran out of the house.

At pet-friendly Bow-Meow Books in Rehoboth Beach, Delaware, it was a lazy August morning. The four-legged staff, all rescues, were amusing themselves by testing their powers of observation on the early customers. Sherlock, a rare dun-brown whippet, was a master of deduction with a keen nose. His faithful companion, Watson, was an all-white bull terrier. Watson was not clever, but he was stout of heart and could always be counted on for muscle. Hercule was Sherlock's equal in brains but was prone to distraction when grooming. He was a fastidious grey Persian with a white mustache and tummy. Lastly, Jane was an older calico of no pedigree. Her specialty was observing how a person or animal behaved to determine their psychology. She had honed this skill living for years among a community of barn cats in Fort Meade, Maryland.

Watson began the analysis. "I say he's a dog's human."

"Why do you say that?" Jane asked, as the athletic, young man walked directly toward the front desk and got in line. "He has a gentle poise. Notice how gracefully he walks."

"He reminds me of my old human," said Watson.

"Not very scientific, old friend," said Sherlock. "Single men are more likely to favor dogs, and I observe the absence of a wedding ring. Not all married men wear rings, but I think we can safely assume he is single, as any wife would have long ago discarded that tattered garment he's wearing."

"I say he's a dog's human based on what appears to be a long, white hair clinging to his derriere," said Hercule. "We cats have fur, not hair, and any self-respecting cat would have deposited much more fur on his human than that."

"Still," observed Sherlock, "there's no substitute for a good sniff." With that, he walked over and put his head near the man's leg and shoes. Returning after a pat and a scratch, he declared, "Definitely a dog's man. His dog is a female, and he feeds her a grain-free, small-breed formula with tuna. The little Maltese in the cage next to me used to eat something similar. I hate that smell. It reminds me of the shelter."

"How on earth do you know what she eats just by smelling her human's shoes?" asked Watson.

"She drools—probably naps on them," answered Sherlock.

"From his scent, I can also tell the man ate sausage pizza from Spicoli's recently. I've made a study of food smells, and Spicoli's sausage is unique in Rehoboth for their use of Jamaican allspice. My old human used to take me tracking. I won every competition save one. Lost to a setter named Irish Adelaide, a remarkable female. Out of respect, she will always be known to me as 'The Bitch.'"

Jane tried to predict the man's preference in books. "I'm having a hard time getting a read on him. He just seems upset. Maybe self-help, but I wouldn't bet on it."

"I did smell adrenaline," said Sherlock.

When the man's turn came for his "audience" with the owners of the store, "Her Majesties Victoria and Regina, the Empresses of India Ink," as they were known to their animal subjects, he put his hands a foot apart and spoke quickly and nervously.

"Wow. That's a big book," said Watson.

"Non, mon ami. He is relating something about his little white companion," observed Hercule, in between licking his paw and grooming his mustache. "Given his agitation, I surmise they have been separated."

Sherlock leaped to attention. "A case! Watson, on your paws. The game is afoot!"

For the rest of the morning, Jane assessed customers and animals, but didn't pick up anything useful. Sherlock gave everyone a good sniff for signs of the little white dog. Not finding any, he chewed his squeaky pipe to contemplate, while Hercule restored his "little gray furs" with a nap in the sunny windowsill. Watson had named their investigation "The Case of the Missing Maltese." He helped Sherlock until story time, when he had to go to work. Watson treated children suffering from a fear of dogs by sitting adorably as they read stories to him. He liked the petting, and the condition of his patients always improved.

Shortly before "high sun time," known to humans as noon, they got a break in the case. A young woman with a beautiful coat of black head-hair came into the store with a small, white dog sporting a pink leash and collar covered in rhinestones. Jane correctly predicted the woman was headed for the "large human pectorals and mammaries" section. Sherlock went over to say hello. After they each got a good sniff, the little dog turned and pleaded, "Help me."

Sherlock recognized her scent immediately. "That woman is not your human."

"No. My human is lost. I got out this morning to go exploring and he hasn't caught up with me yet."

"Didn't your human provide you with tags?"

"Yes, of course, but they were attached to the most dreadful collar. I mean, if you'd seen it. The first thing I did was scrape it off against the corner of a building."

"Do not distress yourself. My colleagues and I will help you. Does your human eat sausage pizza and display questionable taste in his wardrobe?"

"That's him! Is he here?"

"No, but he was here this morning looking for you."

"Oh, thank DOG! I was afraid I would never see him again. I met this woman this morning. She's very nice, but I prefer a large male as pack leader. Still, she has fabulous fashion sense. The first thing she did was take me shopping. I hope she'll let me keep this outfit."

Sherlock called his cohorts over. Hercule raised an eyelid and said he could hear fine from the windowsill.

"I am Sherlock. Allow me to present Watson and Jane. That is Hercule."

"Is this the missing Maltese we've been looking for?" Watson asked.

The little dog bristled. "Please. I'm a Lhasa apso. Maltese. I mean, really!"

"I forgot to ask your name," said Sherlock.

"Lucy, with my human. However, this woman is calling me–"

As if on cue, the woman took a few steps and gave a tug, "Katniss, over here, honey."

Sherlock said, "The problem is how to find your human. Do you know his name?"

"It sounds like 'Collar,' but I'm not sure. I call him Meal Ticket. I think her name is Walkies, but I only heard it once."

"Not very helpful. Can you describe the area where you last walked Collar?"

"Yes, there were lots of wooden houses with screen porches."

"That describes most of the town. Can you think of anything else?"

"On our walks, I saw a German shepherd, a golden retriever, and a tiny little dachshund."

"Shepherds and retrievers lead their humans on long

walks," said Sherlock. "Even if we find them that doesn't narrow our search. But miniature dachshunds don't stray far from home. Can you describe him?"

"Oh, yes. He's very handsome. Black and brown with a long, luxurious coat. He'd be just my type if he weren't such a pussyfoot. He won't walk unless his human picks him up and carries him away from the house. Then he trots home … looking gorgeous."

From the corner, Hercule perked up an ear. "Ah. No doubt you are referring to Monsieur Hartley, or 'One Way,' as he is known. He's a year-round resident and lives near the noisy place with screaming children and lights that spin at night."

"That's him!" Lucy said.

Just then, book in hand, Walkies made her way to the cash register, pulling Lucy behind her. As they were leaving the store, Lucy pleaded, "Oh, please hurry. The way Walkies has been wrinkling her nose makes me think she wants to give me a bath, and we hardly know each other!"

"Where does Walkies stay?" Jane called after her.

"We're on a street near—"

And with a tug of the leash, she was gone.

Hercule joined Jane and Watson in a huddle around Sherlock as he spoke.

"We have two problems to solve. Where is Collar, and where is Walkies taking Lucy? Watson, you and I need to get onto Lucy's trail before it gets cold. Hercule and Jane, you go find Collar. Then we have to get them both back to the shop at the same time."

As Jane and Hercule made for the cat door, Sherlock went behind the counter with Watson close behind.

"Which one, Sherlock?" asked Watson.

"Regina, I think. She's easier to walk, and I see she's wearing her fang shoes today."

Watson began pushing at Regina's leg, while Sherlock pawed at the leashes hanging on the wall. Regina turned, and from her tone they could tell they had been successful.

Once outside, Regina made her usual turn to the right. Watson started to follow, but Sherlock stopped him. "Not that way, Watson. Our quarry went to the left." Watson stopped on the spot and waited for Regina to reach the end of her leash. Then he turned and began pulling her in the direction of the boardwalk. Teetering on her high heels, she had no choice but to follow.

When they reached the first cross street, the scent became even stronger. Sherlock followed it as far as Basher's but lost it in the maze of sweaty legs and squashed french fries. Sitting down, he said, "I've lost the trail, Watson."

Watson sat next to him. Regina pulled on Watson's leash, but it might as well have been tied to a lamppost.

Thinking out loud, Watson said, "They can't have gone on the wooden street—no dogs allowed. And they can't have just disappeared."

"Watson, old boy, you've done it again. Once you eliminate the impossible, whatever remains, no matter how improbable, must be the truth. Lucy brought Walkies here to get fries, then doubled back. That's why the scent was stronger after we crossed the street."

They were off again, retracing their steps back to the corner, where they turned right. Little Regina was being dragged unsteadily behind Watson's sturdy gait as though she had harpooned a whale. Away from the big double street, with its heavy concentration of smells, it was a snap for Sherlock to follow the scent. After turning this way and that, the trail finally led up a front walk.

As they approached, Lucy gave a yelp from the screened in porch. "However did you find me?"

"Alimentary, my dear girl," said Sherlock. "You eat a lot of tuna fish."

As he and Jane went out the cat door to the alley, Hercule said, "Shall we proceed to the noisy place to find Monsieur One Way?"

Jane had the beginning of an idea, so she bathed her paw to think. After a moment she said, "We could search, but I think I begin to understand Mr. Collar. It's almost 'high sun time,' and he does not have a female. Odds are good his refrigerator is empty, so he will need to find sustenance."

"Jane, my wise friend. You suggest we watch the dining establishments? A good thought, but there are so many. How will we choose?"

"He's dressed rather humbly for any of the finer restaurants, and I suspect he will want something he can eat while he continues his search."

"And we know he likes ze pizza," said Hercule.

"Spicoli's!" they said in unison and began racing in that

direction. After agreeing on a plan, they took up positions on either side of the door. They didn't have to wait long before Jane spied Collar in his torn T-shirt.

"Hercule, he's coming."

"Mon Dieu! It is too soon. Our friends will need more time. We must wait before we act."

Per Sherlock's instructions, Watson marched up to the screen door, dragging Regina behind him. With his paw, he ripped open a gash large enough for Lucy to jump through. As soon as she was out, Sherlock bit his leash and pulled it out of Regina's hand. Then, Sherlock and Lucy took off running. Watson, despite Regina's pulling and pleading, planted himself in front of the door and, doing his darndest to look mean, kept Walkies inside. Several bystanders tried to catch Lucy, but Sherlock moved in serpentine fashion around her as they ran. Once his two friends had a good head start, Watson turned around, yanked his leash out of Regina's hand, and sprinted back to the shop.

About the time Collar entered Spicoli's, Jane and Hercule heard a commotion and turned to see the madcap chase on the opposite sidewalk: Sherlock clearing the way for Lucy, Watson close behind, and the two women doing their best to catch up. Time was now of the essence, and Jane and Hercule waited anxiously outside Spicoli's for Collar to exit.

Finally, Collar grabbed a bag and turned toward the door. Jane got into position, and just as Collar stepped out, she ran squarely into his legs and let out a convincing screech of pain. She lay there for a moment, feigning injury, and then slowly got up, holding out one of her front paws and limping.

As they had hoped, Collar made soothing sounds and bent down to read her tag. Then, he scooped her up in his free arm and began walking toward the store.

Out of breath and frantic, Regina and Walkies ran to the bookstore, where they were met at the door by Victoria.

"Whatever happened? Sherlock and Watson just showed up barking at the door with this little, white dog."

A few feet inside the store, Sherlock was sitting up, looking regal as if nothing had happened, while several yards back, poor little Lucy was flat on her belly, panting furiously. Watson, also panting, had placed himself between Lucy and the door.

Stepping forward, Walkies exclaimed, "Katniss, thank goodness you're safe."

As she approached, Watson stood, showing his teeth and growling softly, stopping her in her tracks.

Regina ran over and grabbed Watson's collar. "Watson, what's gotten into you?" She then turned to Walkies. "Don't worry, he looks fearsome, but he's just a big puppy dog." Regina tried to pull Watson toward his crate in the back of the store, but he stayed rooted to the spot.

"We are so sorry," said Victoria. I can't imagine what's gotten into Sherlock and Watson, chasing your little dog like that."

"Thank you, but she's not mine. I wish she were. I found

her wandering around lost this morning. She's so sweet I couldn't bring myself to take her to the shelter, so I called them and left my number. I bought this cute collar so I could walk her around and look for her owner."

"No luck, clearly. And no one called?"

"Someone may have. Like a dummy, I forgot to charge my phone last night and it died sometime this morning. I've had so much fun walking her around town that a part of me hopes no one ever calls."

"I don't blame you, but I think I know who her owner is. There was a guy here this morning looking for a little, white dog just before you came in. The way you've got her all blinged-out, I never imagined it could be the same dog."

Just then the door opened and in strutted Hercule. Behind him was Collar, with a paper bag in one hand and Jane draped over the other arm like a furry football. He saw Victoria and walked over.

"Hi, I'm Colin—I was in here earlier looking for my dog. I'm really sorry, but I stumbled over your cat. I think I hurt her paw."

Safely home, Jane hopped down and began rubbing against his leg with no sign of injury. Upon hearing her human's voice, Lucy let out a happy bark and ran up to him wagging her tail.

"There you are, you rascal!" Colin got on one knee and set down the bag as Lucy jumped into his arms, licking his face profusely. "Where have you been, girl, and where did you get that collar?" Then, he held her up out in front of him and said in his best Ricky Ricardo voice, "Lucy, you've got some 'splaining to do!" Standing, he asked, "Who do I have to thank for taking such good care of Lucy?"

A blushing Walkies shyly raised a gently waving hand. "That would be me. Hi, I'm Whitney."

Victoria politely excused herself and resumed her position behind the counter. Regina was busy rubbing Watson's tummy, as he had rolled over the moment Colin had come into the store.

"Thank you very much," said Colin. He returned Lucy to the floor, and she lay down with her head on Whitney's shoes. "She seems to like you."

"And I adore her. Such a sweetie pie. Honestly, I was hoping she was a stray so I could keep her."

"That's what I was afraid of. The shelter gave me a number, and I've been calling all morning, but no one ever picked up. I guess that was you."

"Yes, I'm sorry–my phone died."

"It happens. Excuse me a second. Let me get rid of this." Colin picked up the bag holding his uneaten takeout and walked over to a trash can. Then he walked back, smiling. "I'm kinda hungry. Can I buy you lunch as a thank-you?"

"That'd be great," said Whitney, running her hand through her hair. "Just let me go home first and change. I chased after Katniss—sorry, Lucy—for blocks. I must be a mess."

"If that's a mess, I can't wait to see you put together." He smiled and looked down. "Seems I could use a change, too."

"Shall we meet back here in an hour?"

"Sounds good. If there's any problem, I'll call you."

"And I'll answer this time!"

Lucy trotted over to Watson and licked his face. "My big, strong terrier." She seemed about to say more, but Colin picked her up and carried her out of the store.

A few minutes later, with Jane on her perch by the door and Hercule napping on the windowsill, Watson walked over to Sherlock.

"Well, Sherlock, another successful case."

"Thank you, Watson. I couldn't have done it without you."

"Your brains and my brawn, eh?"

"Precisely. But now I am again faced with the tedium of existence. Watson, I must have a case!"

"How about The Case of the Missing Milk-Bone?"

"You never tire of that one, do you, old friend? Very well."

They walked over to their queens, Victoria and Regina, and began pushing hard against their legs. Victoria held their collars while Regina took two treats and stalked out into the store, looking for a good hiding place. Upon her return, Sherlock leaped to attention. "A case! Watson, on your paws. The game is afoot!"

Doug Harrell has spent much of his life in Delaware. In high school, he read Sherlock Holmes stories and Agatha Christie novels with a black cat named Midnight on his lap. Doug and his late wife, Carolyn, were the humans of orange tabby cat brothers named Sherlock and Watson, who spent a lot of their long lives detecting food and warm laps. When Doug met his wife, Michelle, he fell in love with her and with her orange tabby cat, Mr. (Mario) Lemieux. Although Mr. Lemieux wasn't so sure about Doug, before long they were best buddies.

Doug and Michelle now live with their three orange tabby cats (are you sensing a pattern here?): Raymond, Robert, and Frankie. Raymond, Robert, and Frankie send their love to Aunt Jane and the other nice humans at Faithful Friends Animal Shelter who took such good care of them before they found their forever home.

The Heart Bandit

By Jeanie P. Blair

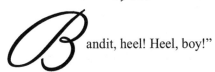andit, heel! Heel, boy!"

Evan Sheppard heard the frantic commands of the young woman chasing the puppy that was racing toward him. He jumped out of his pickup truck and crouched down to intercept the furry escapee, who leapt into his arms. Evan chuckled as the excited pup panted and licked his face from top to bottom.

"Oh, my gosh. Thank you for grabbing him." The woman came to a halt, her blonde ponytail flapping behind her. She cupped the puppy's face in her hands. "Bad boy!" The dog playfully nipped at her hands, then commenced licking his new friend's chin. "I'm sorry. He's usually pretty obedient."

"No worries. He's adorable." Evan couldn't help but be a little mesmerized by the woman's stunning green eyes.

The woman smiled and extended her hand. "I'm Casey Lockwood."

He clutched her hand. "Evan Sheppard. Nice to meet you."

"Likewise. And this is Bandit, which I'm sure you've already gathered."

Evan smiled. "Love the name. I assume you named him that because of his markings?"

Bandit was mostly white, with one brown splotch on his back and another that masked his eyes.

"Thanks. Well, it was mainly because he stole my heart as soon as I saw him. His mask—and the fact that my socks keep disappearing—also helped."

Evan chuckled. "Ahh. He's an ornery one, huh?"

Casey smiled. "Oh, yeah."

Evan scratched the pup's ears. "He's a bulldog, right?"

"Actually, he's a bull pug—a bulldog-pug mix. He's a rescue from a puppy mill."

"Aww. Poor guy. Thank goodness for rescues."

"Absolutely." Casey pointed to the slate-blue duplex behind them. "Do you live here?"

"Yes. Just moved in this week."

"Oh. Did you buy the place? I knew the owner—Elsie Carlisle. What a nice lady." She ceased her inquisition. "I'm sorry. None of my business."

Evan smiled. "Actually, I *did* buy the house from Elsie. She's my aunt. Maintaining two homes became too much for her. But she loves this place, so I figured if I bought it, she could still enjoy it anytime she wants."

"That's really nice. Well ..." Casey reached out and retrieved her little runaway from Evan. "Time to get this munchkin some dinner. Thanks again for intercepting him. Please give my love to Elsie."

"Will do." Evan smiled. "Nice meeting you both."

"Same here." Casey turned and made her way back down the block.

Evan couldn't resist taking a few lingering glances as she walked away. She had a runner's physique, and he smiled, thinking she'd need it to keep up with that energetic pooch of hers.

Casey locked the door of her Rodney Street bungalow. She set Bandit down, and he raced to the kitchen. Casey laughed. "I swear, you *must* have a little doggie watch hidden somewhere." Bandit yapped, wagging his nubby tail while she opened his kibble. As she filled his bowl, she thought about her handsome, new neighbor. His dark-brown hair made his steel-blue eyes pop, but not as much as his sexy side-smile. *He can't be single. A guy like that couldn't possibly be un-attached.*

Casey sipped her morning coffee while she reviewed the lessons for her first appointment. Becoming a professional tutor was the best decision she'd ever made. After a decade in the classroom, she decided that tutoring and mentoring the kids in need of extra help and encouragement was much more rewarding.

Casey looked at her kitchen clock. The Masons were usual-ly on time. Danny's overbearing "smother" saw to that, which Casey felt contributed to Danny's academic shortcomings. Bandit adored Danny, but often greeted his mother with a muffled growl. Casey was always amazed by Bandit's keen instincts.

As soon as her appointments were finished, Casey tossed her backpack into her Jeep, strapped Bandit into his doggie seat, and headed for the Rehoboth Animal Rescue. Her best friend, Rachel, owned the shelter, and Casey loved volunteering whenever her schedule allowed.

Casey pulled into a parking spot, then turned to Bandit. "OK, munchkin, promise Mommy you'll be a good boy today." The pup agreed via a couple of cheerful yaps as Casey grabbed her backpack, unlatched him, and hopped out of the SUV.

Once inside, Casey let Bandit loose. He was always obedient while they were there. She greeted the receptionist, who told her Rachel was feeding the dogs. As Casey and Bandit neared the kennels, the sounds of hammering and power tools resonated through the aisles. Bandit stopped, threw his nose in the air, and darted down the aisle and around the corner. Casey gave chase, calling after him. As she rounded the corner, she came to an abrupt halt and gasped. Bandit was once again in the arms of Evan Sheppard. And what a set of arms they were—completely exposed this time—in the black muscle shirt he was wearing.

"Well, hey there," Evan said, flashing his sexy smile. "I assume you're looking for this little fugitive?"

Casey struggled to peel her eyes from his biceps. "Uhh … yes, I am." She frowned at Bandit and playfully grabbed his flappy little jowl. "What am I going to do with you?"

"He must've heard the commotion. He's just a curious little dude, that's all."

Casey rolled her eyes. "So it seems."

"So, what brings you here? Looking for a buddy for this guy?" Evan scratched the pup's wrinkly chin.

"No. Actually, I volunteer here."

"Oh. That's great."

"How about you?"

"Rachel hired me to make some repairs and replace a section of fencing. Her grandmother is good friends with Aunt Elsie. She referred me."

"Oh, so you're a contractor?"

"Yep. Left the corporate world about six years ago, flipped some houses, then decided to make the permanent move down here. Aunt Elsie was ready to sell, so it was perfect timing."

More perfect than you know. "Cool. Well, I'd better go. Have you seen Rachel?"

"I think she's in the next aisle."

Casey took Bandit from the hefty arms corralling him. "Well, thanks for capturing him again."

"No problem. Nice to see you again." Evan winked at her.

"Same here." Casey blushed.

Evan let out a chuckle, which she assumed was due to her pink cheeks. Flustered, she made a quick exit to go find her friend.

"Rachel!"

"Hey, girl!" The two hugged. Rachel touched noses with Bandit, who slathered her with kisses. "Hi, pumpkin! Auntie Rachel missed you!"

"Aww, he missed you, too." Casey reattached Bandit's leash and set him down on the floor.

"Since when do you leash him here?"

"Since he's been a bad boy."

"What?"

"As soon as I unleashed him, he bolted to your contractor."

Rachel grinned. "Oh. So, you've met Evan, huh?"

"Yes. Well, actually, I met him yesterday."

"*Really?*" Rachel said, with exaggerated surprise.

"Don't go there, Rachel. No matchmaking."

"I have no idea what you're talking about."

"Yes, you do. And you promised."

"Aww, c'mon. You're as bad as Ronny. He said the same thing."

Perhaps the only person who knew Rachel as well as Casey was Rachel's husband, Ronny.

"Good. Ronny's right."

"Oh, fine." Rachel pouted. "I just hate that you're alone."

"I'm *not* alone. I have Bandit … and you and Ronny."

Rachel rolled her eyes. "You know what I mean."

"Rach, I know you mean well, but I'm fine. And you know I'm done with relationships."

Bandit groaned and lay down on the cement floor, face between his paws.

"I'm sorry, Case, but just because Brad was a giant schmuck, doesn't mean all guys are. Evan seems like a genuinely nice guy. Aaand … he's single."

"How do *you* know? Did you ask him?"

"Don't look so horrified. Of course not. My grandma asked his aunt."

Casey gasped. "That's just as bad!"

"Relax. She didn't mention your name."

"I should hope not! And she'd better not. That goes for *you* too."

Rachel threw her hands in the air. "OK, OK. I give up. You win."

"Great. Glad we cleared that up. Now I can get some book-keeping done. Need any help before I go?"

"No, thanks. I'm almost done."

"OK." Casey turned and headed to her office, Bandit trotting close behind.

Casey's rumbling stomach indicated it was time for lunch, and time for Bandit to have a potty break. She giggled at her baby, who was on his back, snoring like a drunken sailor. She tickled Bandit's chubby little potbelly. "Hey, itty bitty. Rise and shine."

Bandit's eyes opened and he gave a big yawn.

"Wanna go outside?"

With that, Bandit was off his bed, tail wagging, waiting for Casey to latch him up. She opted to harness him, since some of the fencing might be down. She grabbed her lunch from her backpack, and they headed to the yard. When she stepped outside, Casey noticed Evan, leaning against the wall, talking on his cell phone.

"Cool. Pizza and bowling sounds great. I'll see you around six o'clock. We'll see about spending the night." He paused. "Love you too, sweetheart."

Casey felt an unexpected wash of disappointment. *So much for being unattached.*

Not wanting Evan to catch her eavesdropping, Casey darted toward the gazebo in the far corner of the yard, struggling with Bandit, who began yapping and pulling his lead in the other direction when he saw Rachel emerge with several other dogs. Casey saw that the old fencing was still intact, so she let him loose to greet his pals. Bandit shot off like a rocket, but to her surprise, he bypassed the other pups and made a beeline for Evan. Bandit barked at Evan, but every time he reached down to greet the pup, Bandit ran a few steps toward the gazebo.

"What's up, you crazy pooch?" Evan said playfully.

Bandit continued inching toward the gazebo, staying just out of Evan's reach.

Evan called to Casey. "I think he's inviting me to lunch— OK if I join you?"

What was with Bandit's obsession with Evan? "Absolutely." *Awkward.*

Evan settled in on the opposite side of the picnic table with his lunchox. Casey poured some of her bottled water into a travel bowl for Bandit and set it on the gazebo floor.

"This is nice," Evan said. "Great place to relax in the shade."

"Yeah, I love it. I always eat lunch here on nice days."

Bandit finished drinking and stared up at Casey, not-so-patiently awaiting his daily nibbles of carrot.

"I'm really sorry. Bandit's obviously obsessed with you." Casey said.

Evan laughed out loud. "What can I say? I have that effect on people," he joked. "And on dogs, too, it seems."

"Really? *Do* tell."

Evan laughed. "I'm kidding. Just the opposite, actually."

Casey was wide-eyed. "Seriously?"

"Seriously." Evan frowned. "Why are you surprised?"

Because you're so hot. "Umm, well, because you just don't strike me as someone who's shy, that's all."

"My dad was in the military, so we moved a lot when I was little. I never had a chance to make lasting friendships. I was always the new kid. And I was chubby. The chubby, new kid was *never* the popular kid."

The sadness in his eyes made her chest ache. "That's awful."

Bandit whimpered, so Casey put her hand down to pet him and he lay back down.

"He finally took a permanent post when I was in high school. I joined the football team and lost weight, but I still wasn't confident enough to ask girls out."

"I'm sorry, Evan." She fought the urge to jump up and hug him.

"Ahh, it's all good. I dated some in college, then, a few years after, I met the love of my life."

"Oh, that's great." Casey swallowed. *Ouch.*

"Yeah. I thought so, too." Evan stared at the table and grimaced. "Until she left me at the altar—in front of two hundred of our closest family and friends."

"Oh, Evan." Casey reached out and placed her hand on his. "I'm so sorry."

Evan looked at Casey and pulled his hand from under hers. "Yeah, well, I'm over it. But no more serious relationships for me."

Bandit looked up at Evan and let out an audible sigh.

Evan checked his watch. "Well, I'd better get back to work." He combed his fingers through his wavy hair. "Listen, I'm sorry. That's not something I usually talk about."

"No problem, Evan. If it's any consolation, I can relate."

"I'm sorry to hear that. Maybe you can tell me your horrible story sometime."

"Maybe," Casey said. Though it wasn't something she liked to relive.

Evan stooped and patted Bandit's head. "Thanks for the invite, little buddy." He stood and turned to Casey. "Thanks again."

"You're welcome. See ya." Casey watched Evan walk away. *Hmm. Was the girl on the phone just a booty call? But he'd told her he loved her. So, did that mean he's one of those bitter guys who's only interested in love 'em and leave 'em revenge relationships?* Wow. She hadn't seen that coming. But better to find out now.

During the next couple of months, Casey saw less of

Evan at the shelter, as his work there had wrapped up. They still exchanged waves from down the block and had an occasional curbside chat. They even shared strolls on the beach with Bandit, trying to train him to not eat every foreign object he found in the sand.

Rachel told her Evan had ended up donating all his work at the shelter. He really *was* a good guy. Shame he had such a tainted opinion of love and relationships. Casey laughed at herself. She had her nerve. She had sworn off relationships, too. But, if she was being honest with herself, Evan was the kind of guy she could imagine herself with. *Bummer.*

Casey was fixing a salad for dinner when there was a knock on the front door. Bandit mustered up his most ferocious bark, which turned to a happy yelp the instant Casey opened the door. There stood Evan, holding up a psychedelic rubber ball.

"Hi. I believe this belongs to you?"

"Hey," Casey replied. "Please, come in." As Evan brushed past her, she got a whiff of him. *Damn he smells good.* "That's Bandit's. How did you end up with it?"

Evan shrugged. "It was in my tool tote."

"How the heck did it get in there?"

"Beats me. But I remembered seeing Bandit with it, so I knew it was his."

"Yes, it's his favorite toy, in fact. I can't imagine how it got into your bag." Casey frowned at Bandit.

Bandit hung his head.

Casey tried her best to be serious. "Bandit!"

The pup's tail vibrated nervously.

Evan laughed out loud, and Casey couldn't contain her amusement.

Casey sighed. "I'm so sorry. He must have seen your bag at the shelter and known it was yours by the scent."

"No problem. I just thought he might be missing it."

"Well, thanks for bringing it down."

Evan turned toward the door.

"Wait. Would you like to stay for dinner?" *What? Where did that come from?*

"Oh, thanks. But I'd hate to impose."

No backsies now. "It's no imposition. Nothing fancy. I was just making a salad, and I have a nice baguette for garlic bread."

Bandit darted over and stood between Evan and the door. He let out an emphatic bark.

"Actually, that sounds nice."

"Great." Casey motioned to Bandit. "I don't think you have a choice, anyway."

Evan looked at Bandit and laughed. "I think you're right."

The two strolled to the kitchen, with Bandit at their heels. Casey poured two glasses of pinot grigio as Evan took a counter stool, and the two chatted while she finished whipping up a lemon vinaigrette and toasting the baguette.

Casey grabbed the salad and said, "It's a beautiful night. Let's eat on the screened porch."

Evan followed her. "It's really beautiful out here. Very tranquil."

"Thanks. It's my favorite part of the house. It's where I come to decompress."

As they enjoyed their dinner, the two shared information about their families and their childhood memories of summers in Rehoboth.

Evan took his last bite, then set down his fork. "That was delicious. You should seriously consider bottling and selling that dressing."

"Really? Wow, thanks!"

"Thank *you*."

"You're welcome."

A strange expression overcame Evan's face.

"Is something wrong?" Casey asked.

"No." Evan paused. "I was just wondering …"

"Wondering what? Evan, what is it?"

He sighed. "I was just wondering what happened in your last relationship."

Casey was in mid-sip and nearly choked on her wine. "Oh, that."

"I'm sorry. I don't mean to pry—I just can't imagine anyone hurting you." Evan's expression turned to a scowl and the muscles in his chiseled jaws tightened.

"It's OK. You shared your nightmare. My turn." Casey took a gulp of wine, then a deep breath. "Brad and I were together for five years. We had discussed our future, but he always had some bullshit justification for putting off a wedding. My friends and family urged me to end it, but I was too naïve to listen. On the fifth anniversary of our first date, Brad called and said he had something important to discuss with me. I was so excited; I thought he was *finally* going to propose." Casey stared down at the table and shook her head. She took another deep breath and swallowed hard.

Evan reached across the table and laid his hand on hers. "Stop. You don't have to continue."

She forced a smile. "I'm OK." She took another deep breath. "Brad arrived and told me to sit on the couch. I thought he was about to get down on one knee, but instead he told me it was over. He said he'd met someone else and was moving to Florida to be with her." She closed her eyes and shook her head. "I swear it felt like someone had zapped me with a taser. He said he was sorry, then walked out. That was two years ago, and I haven't seen or heard from him since."

"Oh, God. Casey. I'm really sorry." Evan tightened his grip on her hand.

"How could I have been so stupid?"

Bandit whimpered as he scooched over and laid his head on Casey's foot.

Evan took both of her hands in his. "You listen to me. That bastard didn't deserve you. You're *much* better off without him, trust me."

"I haven't dated anyone since. That wasn't my only bad relationship, but it *was* my worst. And, I promised myself it would be the last."

"Wow," Evan said with an eye roll. "We really know how to pick 'em, don't we?" He smirked.

Casey couldn't help but let out an anxious chuckle. "Yeah. We sure do."

She stood and began collecting the dirty dishes. Evan helped her carry everything to the kitchen. They made quick work of the post dinner clean-up. Casey wiped the counter, turned to speak to Evan, and the two bumped chests. Evan's piercing eyes locked onto hers. "Oh, gosh. I ... I'm sorry."

Evan held her gaze. "I'm not," he whispered. He reached up to brush a wisp of hair from her face and leaned in to kiss her.

Casey stepped back. "Umm, would you like some gelato?" She could feel herself getting flushed.

Evan smiled, seemingly amused at her embarrassment.

She glowered at him. "I'm glad my awkwardness amuses you."

"I'm sorry. I wasn't making fun of you. I thought it was adorable."

"Adorable? *Really*?"

"Yes. Very."

"Look, Evan. I'm not going to be one of your revenge dates."

"Revenge dates? What are you talking about?"

"I heard you on the phone with your *sweetheart*. You told her you loved her. And now your hitting on me?"

Evan looked confused. "My *sweetheart*?"

"Yes. You were talking about having pizza ... and going bowling ... and possibly spending the night."

Evan rolled his eyes. "That wasn't a girlfriend, Casey. That was my cousin's daughter. They live north of Dover.

Sometimes, when I visit them, I spend the night. I don't get to see them often."

His eyes were locked on hers. He didn't even blink. *He's telling the truth.* "Evan. I'm sorry. I shouldn't have assumed—"

"It's OK. I understand. I should be the one apologizing for coming on so strong. But I'm not going to apologize for the way I feel about you." He paused. "I think I'm falling in love with you, Casey."

Her eyes filled. She didn't realize how much she'd wanted to hear that word again—until now. But she couldn't risk getting hurt again. "Oh, Evan. I'm sorry. But I just can't." A tear rolled down her cheek.

Evan put his hands on her shoulders. "Casey, listen to me. I know you're scared. I was, too, until I realized something. We were both on the receiving end of a really shitty deal. But we're not *those* people. That's why we're meant to be together. I think you feel it, too." Evan gestured toward Bandit, who was standing right beside them, his little head swaying back and forth as they talked, like he was watching a tennis match. "Dogs can sense things, right?"

"Yes. Why?" Casey sniffled.

"Who do you think brought us together? Bandit ran to me out front—that's how we met. He connected us again at the shelter. Then, he coaxed me toward you at the gazebo. And what about the ball in my tool bag? Those weren't coincidences." Evan wiped her tears.

Casey's jaw dropped. "Oh, my God. You're right!" She looked down at Bandit.

"I *am* right. It was Bandit who brought us together. He sensed it from the very beginning, didn't you, boy?"

Bandit barked, jumping and spinning around on his hind legs.

"Oh, Evan." Casey threw her arms around his neck.

Evan took her face in his hands and gave her a tender, lingering kiss.

When they parted, Casey looked into Evan's eyes. "Well, one thing's for sure."

"What's that?"

"I sure did name him correctly. He stole my heart, and then he stole yours for me."

"He sure did," Evan said. "Our little heart bandit."

A native Delawarean, Jeanie Pitrizzi Blair resides in Newark with her husband, Sam, and their miniature schnauzer, Sophia. Jeanie has possessed a love for reading, writing, and the English language since she was a child, which she largely attributes to her grade school English teachers. Though she works full time as an office administrator, Jeanie continues to pursue her dream of becoming a successful romance novelist. She would like to thank her family and friends for their continued support and encouragement. This is her fifth short story published by Cat & Mouse Press. This story is dedicated to Miss Sophia, to all rescue pets that are true blessings to their forever families, and to Grass Roots Rescue and all other rescues and shelters that tirelessly and selflessly save those precious angels every day.

Falling Into Place

by Nancy Powichroski Sherman

*C*laire hobbled on crutches past the brindled greyhound reclining in the sun that poured though the
wall of windows overlooking the beach of North Ocean City,
Maryland. She didn't acknowledge the dog that rested on an
immense corduroy pillow. Why should she? She didn't want
to be here, dog sitting a skinny, long-legged, aloof greyhound
for some friends of her parents.

They had insisted she take on this challenge, referring to it
as a three-day change of scenery. Their close friends Kenny
and Mike had provided the Ocean City condo (and the dog).
Sure, it was nice having an ocean view and spending time
alone without her parents hovering around her, treating her as
a child rather than a nineteen-year-old college athlete. Since
the hard cast had been removed from her left leg and replaced
by a soft brace, they had badgered her several times a day to
go for walks as instructed by her orthopedic surgeon.

Why couldn't they see that her job this weekend was not a
perfect fit? First of all, she had no past experience with household pets—dogs, cats, or even goldfish—to which Kenny had
responded, "That's OK. Patch doesn't have any experience with
you, either," laughter following, good-natured yet annoying to
Claire. And then there was the issue of her current restricted

mobility. Sure, the soft brace was the next step to rehabilitation, but she was reluctant to put aside the crutches and hesitant to put any weight on her left leg. Yet this dog had a regimented schedule, which included four walks each day. Hadn't Kenny or her parents considered the difficulty of performing this task, considering that she needed both hands to use her crutches? Kenny had reassured her that he and Mike had been working with Patch on a lead. "He'll stay by your side—probably," again followed by a laugh. "And if you truly need help, I've left the phone number of our neighbor Aidan; he's good with dogs and has occasionally walked Patch when Mike and I were working late." Then why didn't they ask this neighbor to dog sit?

Now that Kenny and Mike had gone to the Salisbury Airport to catch a flight to Florida for an international conference on greyhound advocacy, their condominium felt strange and a bit uncomfortable, with Claire and Patch at opposite ends of the great room as though neither of them knew quite what to do with the other. Patch remained on his pillow, resting his body—but not his eyes. He watched her, as if waiting to see which furniture the young woman would claim. When she chose the overstuffed sofa, the greyhound seemed to accept the territory arrangement and closed his eyes.

Claire placed a pillow under her left leg, then clicked on the flat-screen TV and cycled through the channels, looking for a movie. Her finger froze on the remote when the screen filled with a closeup of an NBC Sports journalist interviewing a member of the US Olympic track team, Lavinia Stonewell, Claire's roommate at London-Smith University. She watched Vinie's face flush with excitement as she answered the journalist's questions about being the newest member on the track team and how it felt to be the replacement for Claire Evensong after Claire tore her right hamstring during the four-hundred-meter race at the US track and field national finals.

"We are a team with a common goal—to win gold for Team USA. Any of us would step up to make that happen." Claire knew that answer by heart; it was the word-for-word reply that was expected of everyone on the team. The journalist continued to shower compliments on the runner. While Vinie's cheeks were bright pink with joy, Claire felt her own cheeks burn with anger.

Quickly she changed the channel. Nature & More Nature was presenting a show about the various types of spiders found in the United States. She hated spiders. More channel clicking, past reality TV shows, soap operas, romance, and even comedies—nothing of interest to her—and landed on a sports network just in time to see a playback of the moment at the national track-and-field competitions when Claire heard a popping sound in her leg and fell on the track in extreme pain.

She shut off the TV, yelled a vulgar epithet, and fell back against the sofa cushions.

Her sudden movement and the loudness of her voice caused the greyhound to startle. He popped his head into the air to see what was happening.

"Get used to it," Claire told the dog. "I'm not a dog lover. No offense. My parents volunteered me for this. You're stuck with me for the rest of the weekend, just like I'm stuck with you."

She couldn't figure out if the greyhound's eyes were staring at her uncommittedly, like a scientist studying some rare specimen, or if Patch was looking upon her with sympathy. For what? For her injury? Why should a dog care that she had worked so hard in her sport to have a chance at the summer

Olympics, only to have it taken from her by Vinie, who was supposed to be her best friend?

Claire moved to the outside deck with great difficulty, leaving her crutches by the sliding doors and hopping on her good leg so she could reach the railing and rest her arms there. She needed the fresh salt air and the sound of the ocean waves touching shore. But mostly, she needed to get away from the TV, despite her curiosity about what the team was doing on this first day of the summer Olympics. To watch the opening day festivities would remind her that she was not only missing the opportunity to medal but also the chance to visit Tokyo.

Tears formed and ran down her cheeks. She didn't try to stop them. Why bother? She had held in so much of her disappointment during the past month while recuperating from surgery on her grade 3 hamstring tear. Crying at home would have brought her loving parents to her side, reassuring her that she'd be eligible for the next Olympic games, that this was just a bump in the road for her, that other runners have come back stronger after a serious tear.

She felt a tiny nudge at her hip that surprised her enough to stop her tears. It was Patch, standing by her side and looking up at her with dark eyes. She tried to ignore him so he'd go back inside the house and leave her here alone to continue her self-pity party. But the greyhound nudged her again.

Claire released a sigh. "You deserve a better dog sitter, Patch."

She heard her cell phone ring. Of course, it was nowhere near her; it was resting on the arm of the sofa. She hopped to the door, grabbed the crutches, and moved as quickly as she could, until one of her crutches caught on the corner of Patch's pillow. She dropped that crutch to avoid tripping but still didn't get to the phone on time. *Damn*!

When she finally reached the phone, she saw that it was a notification rather than a call: Time to walk the dog.

If her "race" to the phone had been difficult, how would she maneuver with her crutches while holding the leash of an animal that might dart around to find its toileting location?

Her eyes scanned the kitchen island for the notebook that Kenny had prepared for her. The directions for walking the greyhound were listed:

(1) Remove a plastic bag from the box on the hall table where we keep Patch's harnesses and leads. Keep it in your pocket until he does his business. Then bag his poop for disposal. *Yuck*!

(2) Put the rainbow harness on Patch and connect the matching six-foot lead. *What the hell is a lead? Did he misspell* leash?

(3) During the walk, keep him on your left. *But I'm right-handed. Did no one think about that before choosing me as the sitter?*

(4) Since he's adjusting to life outside a racing compound, walk him only a mile and then back again. *I'll be lucky if I can walk that far.*

(5) Sometimes greyhounds stop and refuse to budge when they get scared. Patch hasn't done this with us so far, but he might try this on a new walker, so take a few of his favorite treats from the paw-print canister by the sink; use these to encourage him to start walking again. *You've got to be kidding!*

(6) Grab a bottle of water from the fridge in case you or Patch need a drink during the walk. Remember to lock the

door when you leave. A *bottle? Surely, Kenny and Mike don't expect me to share a water bottle with a dog?*

(7) Any problems? Contact Aidan in Unit 4.

She opened her cell phone and tapped the phone number provided at the bottom of the list. The phone rang three times, then played a recorded message: "Busy saving the world. Leave a message, and I'll call you after I've rid Ocean City of the zombie shark that threatens us all. Mwa-ha-ha-ha."

Patch had tilted his head and was listening to the recording.

Sure, the message was creative and might be funny, but not at this moment. Claire waited for the beep. "Hi. I'm Claire. Kenny and Mike told me I should contact you if I need help with their dog. Please call me ASAP."

She waited twenty minutes. No return call. Yet the greyhound kept going to the hallway, then staring back at her with a whimper. Even someone with no pet experience could figure out the dog's situation—Patch needed to relieve himself.

Claire gathered the items listed by Kenny, hoping that "lead" meant "leash," since that was the only item that matched the rainbow harness. She did her best to figure out how to put the harness on Patch, but finally used YouTube to guide her. After a few minutes, the harness was properly in place. She hooked the leash to her belt—maybe not a good idea, but it freed her hands for her crutches. She led the dog out the front door and toward the outdoor elevator that serviced the six, attached, multi-leveled condominiums; only then did she realize that the backpack containing water and treats was still on the hall table. Worse, she couldn't find the condo key.

She leaned against the door and cried tears of frustration.

Her phone dinged in her back pocket. *Please be that Aidan guy!*

But it was Kenny telling her that he and Mike were getting ready to board the plane and wanted to check in with her before takeoff. Claire kept her voice steady but light. "If I misplace the key to the condo, where might I find another one?"

"Aidan has one."

"I called. He's not home." She was positive that they heard the panic in her voice.

"Are you OK, Claire?"

"Of course, I'm OK. Patch and I are starting—" She stopped, realizing Kenny would know she hadn't stuck to the schedule unless she told a tiny fib. "I mean, on the way back from our walk."

"Did the walk go well?"

Another fib. "Yes, it did. It was good. But back to my question: If I can't find the key to the door and Aidan doesn't call back, what should I do?"

"Text him," Kenny said. "He's always checks messages when he's—" This time it was he who hesitated. "Out and about."

Claire heard the sudden stop in Kenny's voice. *One fibber can certainly detect another fibber,* she thought. *What isn't he telling me about this Aidan guy?*

Her reflection on these questions was put aside for the sake of the greyhound's need to visit a patch of grass—now! She managed to get him and herself into the elevator and down to street level.

Upon seeing a grassy space at the end of the block, Patch

pulled hard in that direction. Claire dropped her right crutch to grab the leash attached to her belt. A tug-of-war took place until the greyhound gave up and squatted right there at the entrance to the elevator.

Claire removed the plastic bag from her pocket and bent down with shaky balance to collect the greyhound's deposit. She noted that Patch sat patiently while she did this. Then, when the bag was tied off, he stood, ready to go for the full walk. With the dog on her left, as directed, she searched for a trash can while trying to figure out where a mile's walk would take her on Wight Street.

After she dropped the bag of waste into a trash can, Patch barked once and took off, causing Claire's belt to break and her to fall to the ground. Fortunately, she landed on her good leg rather than the injured one. Panicked—not for herself but for the loose greyhound—she looked down the road and saw a dark-haired guy, twenties maybe, holding Patch's leash while hugging the greyhound, who was licking his face.

As Claire struggled to get up, she heard the guy call out, "Are you OK?" Then he led the greyhound toward her. "You're Claire Evensong," he said.

How did this stranger know her last name, unless he was that neighbor in Unit 4, but why would Kenny or Mike have offered that information? "And you are Aidan?" she asked. "I left a message on your phone."

"Oh. Sorry. I don't answer my cell phone while I'm running." He reached down to help her to her feet.

That was the moment that Claire stopped staring at his handsome face long enough to notice that he was dressed in shorts, a tank top, and running shoes. "Kenny and Mike didn't mention that 'out and about' meant running."

Aidan smiled and blushed a bit. "I'm a recreational runner, not a champion like you."

Claire shrugged. "Me? Not much of a champion. Dog sitting, when I should be..." She stopped before letting herself fall into the self-pity that had caused tears twice already.

"Competing in Tokyo," Aidan finished her thought. "I can only imagine your disappointment."

"I guess you saw the video that went viral."

He shook his head. "I didn't need to. I was watching the livestream of the competition the day you were injured. I saw it in real time. But, back to your phone call. What did you need?"

"Help." She nodded toward one of her crutches still on the ground. "I can't afford to do more injury to my hamstring as it tries to heal, so I need someone to walk Patch. I can do the other dog sitting things, but I'm not ready to walk a dog while still dependent on a pair of crutches. Attaching the leash to my belt was a stupid idea."

"No, it wasn't. It was a creative solution."

She smiled. "Not as creative as your voice-message recording."

"Yeah, I'm a bit goofy," he said.

"Goofy is good. I could use some goofy in my life right now."

As they walked together toward the outdoor elevator, Aidan holding the greyhound's leash, Claire thought about the track team, the girls who were friends as much as teammates, especially Vinie, who shouldn't be held in disdain. It wasn't anyone's fault that a team member had to be replaced, and Claire knew she should be glad her replacement was a roommate and dear friend rather than someone from another college.

When the elevator opened to the third floor, Claire remembered the missing key. "Aidan, somehow, I managed to misplace the door key."

"No problem. I have one." He unlocked the front door and held it open for her.

There, on the hall table, was the backpack with the treats and water bottle, and next to it, the missing key.

Aidan released the greyhound and watched as it ran to its water bowl in the kitchen.

Claire wanted to know more about this knight in shining armor. "Aren't you thirsty, too, after *your* run?" she asked. She opened the fridge and looked inside. "Iced tea, soda, or water?"

"Water," he answered, coming into the kitchen and sitting on a high stool at the counter.

Claire handed him a bottle of spring water and joined him at the counter with a bottle of iced tea for herself. Only then did she realize how difficult and ungraceful it would be to climb onto the stool.

Aidan offered to help, but she declined—pride was at stake. He watched her efforts patiently, then suggested they go out on the deck to enjoy the ocean breeze.

Claire accepted, pretending she didn't know that he had offered her a way to protect her ego.

Seated on the deck chairs, they talked a bit about everything except running, but mostly they talked about Patch, who had joined them and was resting at Aidan's feet.

"He's come a long way since Kenny and Mike brought him here a month ago," Aiden said.

"What do you mean?"

"You don't know his backstory?" Aidan leaned down and rubbed the greyhound's neck. "Patch was about to be euthanized. He had fallen at the first bend of the race, having been slammed by another greyhound—nothing devastating, just a sprain. But his owner, aggravated at losing a chunk of money on the race, followed him to the kennels and beat him with a strap until a volunteer from the greyhound rescue stepped in to save the dog's life. When Kenny and Mike brought Patch here, they addressed his wounds, both physical and emotional."

Claire looked down at the greyhound's peaceful face. For the first time since she'd arrived, she acknowledged a link between them—Patch had been runner, too, and was no longer active in the sport that injured him. And he was handling his recovery much better than she was handling her own. She felt ashamed that she had delayed her own healing by refusing to put down the crutches and walk. "I never realized until now that a dog could have such an immediate positive effect on a person, even when that person isn't a dog lover. Like me. But he has put my own injury into perspective."

"All dogs and cats supply unconditional love."

"Maybe, but Patch is special. He showed acceptance to me even when I was giving him a cold shoulder. It's going to be hard to say goodbye. Maybe I can visit once in a while."

"Kenny and Mike are not keeping Patch; they're fostering him."

"Fostering?"

"They're helping Patch heal and get ready to go to a forever home," he explained.

The news struck Claire. She had just started to bond with this gentle greyhound, and soon she wouldn't get to spend time with him again. "Do Kenny and Mike know who is getting Patch?"

He shrugged. "I don't think so. Patch is still learning to trust people, so it's too soon for him to go to a permanent home." As he saw her face brighten, he added, "Why don't we walk Patch together this weekend?"

"I'd like that."

Of course, she'd accept a chance to spend time with this handsome and kind guy. And she acknowledged that walking would help her work out her postoperative hamstring and keep her fit so she could be ready to run track again. That would certainly alleviate her parents' worries about her future. But she knew it would take more than physical health; she needed to address her mental health, too, just like the team doctor had said to her and her parents. She needed to confront the two *f*'s of leg injury (and neither of them was a curse word): the fear of falling and fear of failing, both more difficult hurdles than strengthening a hamstring. But how could she repair her mental health? She knew the answer, yet dreaded it.

"Yes, to the dog walks, but with one caveat: Would you consider watching the Olympics with me?"

"Are you sure?"

She nodded. "It will be difficult, but by having you and Patch with me, it might not be as bad. And I do need to move forward rather than staying stuck in place."

"I agree. I'll watch the Olympics here *if* you'll let me make dinner for us tonight."

"Really?"

"You think I can't cook? Do you like spaghetti marinara?"

"Love it."

"And I'll bring a chew for Patch."

After Aidan left, Claire showered and changed, wishing she had packed something better than cropped jeans and knit shirts. When she returned to the great room, she was greeted by Patch, who decided it was OK for him to sit next to her on the sofa. She scratched behind Patch's left ear, and he responded with a happy chittering sound.

"You know, Patch, your racing days were ended because you lost a race, but mine were only derailed by this injury. If I work hard, I might be able to compete again." She would start by trying the exercise program her surgeon recommended, and if everything fell into place, she might just become Aidan's running partner.

Nancy Powichroski Sherman's award-winning short stories have been published in literary journals and anthologies. Her collection *Sandy Shorts* was awarded a first places by Delaware Press Association and the National Federation of Press Women in 2015. Her follow-up collection, *More Sandy Shorts*, launched in June 2019. Both stories she submitted for the first Rehoboth Beach Reads book, *The Beach House*, received honors. That was her first introduction to Cat & Mouse Press and Nancy Sakaduski. In addition to writing, Nancy Sherman is a freelance copy editor and proofreader. (Thank you, Nancy Sakaduski, for bringing me into this project as an associate editor.)

Want to write stories for publication?

How to Write Winning Short Stories

Write short stories with confidence after reading this practical guide that includes developing a theme and premise, choosing a title, creating characters, crafting realistic dialogue, bringing the setting to life, working with structure, and editing. Submission and marketing advice is also provided.

The book is perfect for anyone who is considering writing a short story. It will give beginning writers a practical playbook for getting started and help experienced writers build their skills.

Writing is a Shore Thing Online Newspaper

Writing is a Shore Thing is a free weekly roundup of the top writing advice and tips from experts. This paper is packed with useful information on dialogue, character development, setting, and theme, as well as editing, submitting, and getting published. It can be accessed online at www.writingisashorething.com. Subscribers receive an emailed summary when the paper is published each week.

If you enjoyed *Sandy Paws*

Beach Love

From a romance novelist who longs for a love of her own to a woman who finds love in another era, and from a love-struck wrestler to a real-life Cinderella, these characters, young and old, head to the beach to find that perfect someone. *Beach Love* is an anthology of romance stories that take place in Rehoboth, Lewes, Bethany Beach, Ocean City, Fenwick Island, and Cape May.

Beach Pulp

From giant creatures to ghostly specters and from heroic superheroes to hard-boiled detectives, our beach towns are in for a shock. Whether you're a fan of Nancy Drew or Doctor Strange, *The Twilight Zone* or *Dark Shadows,* you'll want to take a bite out of *Beach Pulp*. Stories set in Rehoboth, Bethany, Cape May, Lewes, Ocean City, and Other Beach Towns.

Rehoboth Beach Reads Series

These anthologies are jam-packed with just the sorts of stories you love to read at the beach. Each contains 20-25 delightful tales in a variety of genres, authored by many different talented writers.

More Sandy Shorts

No one captures bad dogs, bad men, and bad luck like Nancy Sherman. Whether it's twin terrors challenging a nanny on the ferry or hula-dancing Yorkies stealing the scene at the Sea Witch Festival, these stories will have you laughing, crying, and wanting more. Sherman captures the essence of Rehoboth Beach, Lewes, Bethany Beach, Fenwick Island, Cape May, and Chincoteague.

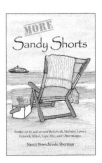

www.catandmousepress.com